Julia Mills

Marrok

Julia Mills

New York Times & USA Today Bestselling Author

Julia Mills

MARROK

A Wolf's Hunger

Julia Mills

Marrok

ACKNOWLEDGEMENTS

Edited by Lisa Miller with Angel Editing Service

Proofread by Tammy Payne with

Book Nook Nuts

Cover Designed by Sassy Queens of Design

Formatted by Charlene Bauer with Wickedly Bold Creations

Julia Mills

DEDICATION

Dare to Dream! Find the Strength to Act! Never Look Back!

Thank you, God.

To my girls, Liz and Em, I Love You. Every day, every way,

always.

To all my readers everywhere, THANK YOU SO VERY MUCH!

Without you, I would be truly lost!

XOXO HAPPY READING!

Author's Note

Wolves? Yep! That's right! I wrote a story about wolves! Whoda thought? LOL, I cannot tell you how exciting it is to be part of A K Michaels' Wolf's Hunger Series. First of all, I simply adore her and secondly, she never ceases to amaze me with her talent, creativity, and genuine kindness.

I am honored to have been asked to be here and cannot wait to hear what y'all think of MARROK. Get ready because this Alpha is H-O-T and his mate is Sassy as all get-out! I fell in love with this couple. Hope you do, too.

So, I'll hush and let you get to it!

Take Care! Happy Reading!

XOXO Julia

Also by Julia Mills

*****

The Dragon Guard Series

Her Dragon to Slay, Dragon Guard #1

Her Dragon's Fire, Dragon Guard #2

Haunted by Her Dragon, Dragon Guard #3

For the Love of Her Dragon, Dragon Guard #4

Saved by Her Dragon, Dragon Guard #5

Only for Her Dragon, Dragon Guard #6

Fighting for Her Dragon, Dragon Guard #7

Her Dragon's Heart, Dragon Guard #8

Her Dragon's Soul, Dragon Guard #9

The Fate of Her Dragon, Dragon Guard #10

Her Dragon's No Angel, Dragon Guard #11

Her Dragon, His Demon, Dragon Guard #12

Resurrecting Her Dragon, Dragon Guard #13

The Scars of Her Dragon, Dragon Guard #14

Her Mad Dragon, Dragon Guard #15

Tears for Her Dragon, Dragon Guard #16

Marrok

Guarding Her Dragon, Dragon Guard #17

Sassing Her Dragon, Dragon Guard #18 (Sassy Ever After Kindle

World)

Kiss of Her Dragon, Dragon Guard #19

Claws, Class and a Whole Lotta Sass, Dragon Guard #20 (Sassy Ever

After Kindle World)

The Dragon with the Girl Tattoo, Dragon Guard #21 (Sassy Ever After

Kindle World)

Her Love, Her Dragon: The Saga Begins, A Dragon Guard Prequel

*****

The 'Not-Quite' Love Story Series

Vidalia: A 'Not-Quite Vampire Love Story

Phoebe" A 'Not-Quite' Phoenix Love Story

Zoey: A 'Not-Quite' Zombie Love Story

Jax: A 'Not-Quite' Puma Love Story

Heidi: A 'Not-Quite' Hellhound Love Story (Magic & Mayhem Kindle

World)

Lola: A 'Not-Quite' Witchy Love Story (Magic & Mayhem Kindle

World)

Sammie Jo: A 'Not-Quite' Shifting Witchy Love Story (Magic &

Mayhem Kindle World)

*****

Kings of the Blood

VIKTOR: Heart of Her King ~ Kings of the Blood ~ Book 1

ROMAN: Fury of Her King ~ Kings of the Blood ~ Book2

ACHILLES: Soul of Her King ~ Kings of the Blood ~ Book 3

*****

CAUGHT: A Vampire Blood Courtesan Romance

*****

MARROK: A Wolf's Hunger

*****

OUT OF THE ASHES: A Zodiac Shifters Paranormal Romance:

Pisces (Guardians of the Zodiac, Book 1)

SCORCHED EMBER: A Zodiac Shifters Paranormal Romance:

Taurus (Guardians of the Zodiac, Book 2)

Gaelic Translations

MARROK: A Wolf's Hunger

A Rabhadh..........Be Warned

Deirfiúr Beag..........Little Sister

Mo Kitten Milís.........My Sweet Kitten

Mo Mac Tíre..........My Wolf

Mo Rí..........My King

Mo Alfa...........My Alpha

Mo Bhanríon.........My Queen

Raibh Aon Rud Riamhálainn Sin...........Nothing was Ever so

Beautiful

Chapter One

Looking out the window, his eyes slowly shifting from left to

 right, Marrok searched the dense underbrush just outside his office window. Tuning out the sounds of the rather arduous debate gaining steam behind him, the Alpha let the sensual

image of the tawny cat float through his mind. Like a clip from

his favorite movie playing on a never-ending loop, he once again

watched with rapt attention as she effortlessly scaled the ridge

just above his favorite spot in the swamp. She was poetry in

motion. Her fluidity and grace indelibly inked upon his

subconscious.

He relived the moment their eyes met. Once again felt the

punch to his gut and the beat of his heart stopping for an

unforgettable split-second in time. He reveled in the fire that

immediately ignited in the depth of his soul. He wanted her,

needed her...*had* to have her. All attempts to push back the insatiable desire to claim her…to mark her as his own, was pointless. The Alpha knew he would make her his…no matter the cost.

Focusing on the giant foxtail and soft rush as it blew in the afternoon breeze, Marrok searched for any signs of the contemptuous female mountain lion he'd chased the night before last.

Chased but not caught…She may have won this battle, but the war rages on…

She'd been trespassing on Gaelach Lán lands, blatantly leaving her scent in a zigzagging pattern for miles, taunting any and all with half a sense of smell to give pursuit. It was unlike any behavior he'd ever witnessed from the neighboring Pride and disconcerting in a way that unsettled the Alpha and left him reeling.

His first thought had been to chase her from Pack lands and report her abhorrent behavior to King Cleander Cattanach, the leader of the mountain lion Pride, but something had stopped him…Something extraordinary…amazing…unbelievably magical.

What had simply been a leisurely run, a way to let his wolf enjoy one of the last cool nights in the Florida swamps before the oppressing heat of the summer was upon them, had turned into the single most defining experience of Marrok's already long life. He'd stopped at one of the many freshwater streams for a drink when his senses were overtaken by the scent of orange blossoms and heavenly female musk. Both man and wolf were forced to stand up and take notice as fire rushed through their veins.

Although feline, the mountain lion's spirit, the true essence of her being, had filled the Alpha with a powerfully hypnotic mix of wanton desire and total completion. It was as if both powerful beings, man, and wolf, were immediately held hostage and forced to watch the lioness stalk their lands as if she owned them.

Marrok

Without thought or reason, he'd quickly abandoned the idea of chasing her away and followed instead. He was amazed at how easily she made her way across trails, avoided traps, and wound around intentional overgrowth that he and his father had created and claimed for their Pack many years ago. Marrok was dumbfounded by her complete confidence and the air of superiority with which she surveyed *his* land. At times, the lioness was so elegant and sure-footed that even the Alpha had struggled to keep up.

But then the wind changed course, once again bathing him in her sweet scent; the delicious aroma of warm feline and fresh air. It was as if the true spirit of *home* was permeating every strand of his thick auburn fur. There was no doubt Destiny wanted him to give pursuit, feared that if he lost sight of *her,* the Alpha would also lose sight of his one chance for happiness, fulfillment...*love*.

Their game of follow-the-leader had gone on for hours, making Marrok wonder where his lioness was leading him or if she even knew herself. And then, as if by design, they had reached the sawgrass marsh, the flatlands where only the very tip of her tail shown above the tall stalks of grass. He followed that bit of white fur shining in the moonlight, musing that never before had he thought of a tail as sexy, but had no doubt it was merely the beginning of discovering that every delectable inch of his mate was all too alluring and absolutely fascinating.

Lost in thought, Marrok had been taken off guard by the sound of a gunshot. Zeroing in on his mate, he'd raced to catch her as she sped through the marsh, stopping only when he reached the border separating Pack and Pride lands. Quickly changing back to human form, the Alpha had opened his preternatural senses as wide as they would go. He searched for the lioness, searched for the origin of the gunshot, searched for signs of danger…but came up empty-handed on all accounts. It was as if the last few hours had been a dream; some sort of mirage his mind had made up to pass the time.

Marrok

Turning on his heel, breathing the cool night air, Marrok once again inhaled the heady scent of orange blossoms as he headed back to his home. His wolf howled in his mind, pining for the feline he knew to be his mate. Calming his beast, the Alpha whispered, *"Never fear, old boy, we'll find her."*

"Dammit, Marrok, are you even listening?" Olivia's bellow pulled the Alpha from his musings a split second before her shoe hit him in the back of the head.

Spinning and bending in one fluid motion, Marrok scooped his sister's shoe off the ground, threw it back at her, and growled, "Never," he took a step forward and growled with even greater menace, *"never,* throw your shoe at me again."

Angus, Olivia's mate, was on his feet and standing between the Alpha and his sister as Olivia's eyes grew large and she put her hands up in surrender. "Sorry, Mar, just playing." Then patting her mate, a centuries-old red dragon, on the back, she whispered, "It's okay, Angus, Marrok won't hurt me."

Maintaining eye contact, the dragon rumbled a curt warning, "*A rabhadh*," in Gaelic, adding, "He'd better not," in English.

Biting his tongue, Marrok worked hard to control his temper as his vision turned red and his wolf's growl shook the confines of his mind. He'd never...*never* snapped at his sister before, not even when she was young and reckless. He'd raised her after the death of their parents, had seen to her every need, even braided her long auburn curls that were just a touch lighter than his own unruly locks. Hell, he'd participated in tea parties and played Barbies. She was the proverbial apple of his eye and had grown into an amazing woman and she-wolf of whom he could not be any prouder. So why, after all these years, was he losing his cool over one of her typical pranks?

Stop denying it...The legends are true...You need to find that cat...

Shaking his head, trying to think of anything but his lioness, the Alpha tried to regain his legendary control. He took several slow, long, deep breaths, counted to ten, but nothing even put a dent in his fury. His irritability…his need…his insatiable hunger for *her* was becoming more than he could handle. It was all-encompassing and completely maddening. The last forty-eight hours had been a living hell. He'd slept less than four hours in total and could do little more than pace the floor.

Taking yet another deep breath, the Alpha stood tall and looked around the table. He saw shock and disbelief at his behavior on every face. His closest confidants looked at him like he'd lost his mind and dammit, maybe he had. Their worry and fear beat at him. Their good intentions exasperated him. Their question of where had his usual good nature and even temper gone infuriated him. Their looks of pity made him want to lash out, to roar…to run from the room, call forth his wolf, and race to *her*, the only one who could calm the war raging inside him.

Glancing at Finn, his long-time friend and Beta, he listened as the words *legendary hunger and torment* floated through the grey wolf's mind. Marrok accepted the concern and need to help coming from the Pack Healer, Mariah, as she remembered witnessing firsthand what The Hunger, as the ancient wolves had called it, could do to an Alpha.

Visions of other wolves, the ones she'd treated during her illustrious career, floated through the mind of the almost millennium old, pure white wolf. Images flipped from one to another like pages in a photo album, each depicting strong, powerful Alphas in the throes of what could only be explained as a mating call of epic proportions. It was rare, only seen in a handful of Alphas throughout the ages, said to affect the 'true and chosen'. There was no rhyme or reason to which of the strongest wolves this debilitating need to have and claim their one true mate affected.

It struck like a thief in the night, signaling the Alpha's mate was near, immediately driving both man and beast to near distraction with need and wanton desire. The longer the wolf was made to go on searching for his mate, the more severe the symptoms became. Some suffered simply sleepless nights combined with the inability to think or eat, while others had hallucinations, mindless bouts of rage, and endless torment. There had been terrible tales of Alphas who, before The Hunger, had been able to control their shift down to a single claw, but once struck by the fable come to life, found themselves uncontrollably flashing from man to wolf and back again. Some roamed the swamps in a stupor, howling, calling out for the one person in all the world that Destiny had designed to complete them body and soul, their one True Mate.

"Let's get back to the treaty with the Blue Ridge Pack in North Carolina. I know Olivia and Angus delivered the paperwork, and I received theirs, but we haven't gotten anything back yet. I had heard they wanted to talk to Barbara and Tristan Wolfe to see how our agreement with them was working out." Finn looked at Olivia, who had been instrumental in getting a treaty established for access to the lands of the Wolfe Pack out west, along with finding her mate only a few months earlier, and asked, "Have you heard anything back from either of them?"

While trying to focus on her answer, Marrok was taken off guard when his Beta suggested, *"If you need to take a minute, I got this,"* through the unique telepathic link they'd shared since childhood.

"I'm fine," Marrok grumbled, narrowing his eyes and clenching his fists.

"I spoke to Ellie, Barbara's daughter, last night. She said her mom and dad had talked to the Blue Ridge wolves and told them we were good people, but for some reason that Ellie couldn't explain, her dad, Tristan, told her to warn me to be careful."

"Maybe we need to take a trip up north and check things out," Finn proposed. "What do you think, Marrok?"

The sound of his name pulled the Alpha back to the present for the umpteenth time. Restless, irritated, and more than fed up with the bureaucratic bullshit he'd been dealing with for most of his life, Marrok slammed his fists on the table, glared at

his, Beta and roared, "I truly do not give one fucking iota!"

Seething with uncontrollable, unexplainable anger, he hit

the table again and again, stopping only when his knuckles sank

into the highly-polished surface and the sound of cracking wood

reached his ears. A red hue, cold and malicious, slowly spread

across his vision as the Alpha stood to his stately seven-foot

height, glowered at his closest and most-trusted confidants, and

growled, "Do. Not. Follow. Me," before turning on his heel and

stalking from the room.

Throwing open the heavy oak doors to the Gaelach Lán

Grande Hall, Marrok's boots hit the first step a second before

magic filled the air and man became beast. The pads of his huge

paws hit the cobblestones of the path leading to the forest as the

wind ruffled his thick auburn coat. Racing over the freshly

mowed Bermuda grass and through the soft-stemmed bulrush,

sending the hanging clusters of tiny yellow flowers flying

through the air, the Alpha ran at full speed for almost an hour, stopping only when he reached his favorite watering hole.

Panting, more tired than he could ever remember being, Marrok flopped down on the banks of the small pond shaded by the enormous coastal willow with its sagging leaves and leaning branches. His eyes slid closed as the soft sound of the water lapping against a fallen log and the song of the tree frogs lulled him to sleep.

Sure he was dreaming, the Alpha let his head roll to the side as soft fingers ran through the thick fur at his neck. Inhaling deeply, he was filled with the sweet, crisp scent of orange blossoms and knew for sure he never wanted to wake up.

Rolling onto his back as the gentle touch moved from his neck down his chest, Marrok's eyes popped open and his heart raced as lips touched the tip of his ear followed by a low, raspy whisper that enticed, "Why not lose the fur coat and come out and play, my big strong Alpha."

Chapter Two

Scotlyn, Scottie to her friends and Pain-in-the-ass to her father,

 knew she shouldn't have gone back to the swamp, knew she was trespassing on Gaelach Lán lands, knew it could only bring more trouble, but absolutely could *not* stay away. Every hour, every minute, damn near every second since running into that obstinate, persistent, and absolutely gorgeous Alpha, she'd been able to think of little else.

Their meeting hadn't been planned or contrived, honestly, hadn't even occurred to her. The lioness and Princess of the Cattanach Pride had been crossing over into the Wolf Pack's land from the time she was able to wear fur. Sure, she'd been caught by the Elder Kilbride and sent home with her tail between her legs more times than she cared to remember, but after he and his wife had passed and Scottie had gotten older, she'd gotten a damn sight better at sneaking in, prowling around, and getting out without anyone ever knowing she'd been there. But then Marrok had happened upon her and things had gotten exponentially more complicated and incredibly exciting.

Thinking back, she had no clue how he'd found her or how he'd been able to track her so easily. Using her powerful magic from the Goddess, Scottie had taken the extra precaution of hiding her scent before ever stepping foot off the lands of her Pride. Her subterfuge had never failed before, but that night it was like the Alpha had supernatural radar and she had been tagged.

At first, she was scared, then intrigued, and after getting a whiff of his deep-woods scent and masculine musk, Scottie had happily led the sexy auburn wolf on an arousing game of catch-me-if-you-can. She could hear her momma's voice as if the great lioness were still alive. *"Scottie, girl, you gotta chase a man until he catches you. Remember, males like to think it was their idea, so if you find one you fancy, you just let him believe he has the upper hand."* The beautiful lioness would wink before going on,

"It doesn't matter what everyone else thinks, you'll know if he's the one for you." Her mother would pull her close and look her in the eye, adding, "It's worked for almost seventy-five years with your father and we are as happy as the day we were mated." The two would hug and laugh until both were out of breath.

"Oh, Mom, I miss you so much," the lioness whispered.

Watching her fingers weave in and out of Marrok's thick fur as if they were committing every strand to memory, Scottie let her mind wander to the time when all her dreams for a happily ever after had been snatched from her grasp, forever lost to the cruel, harsh reality of Pride business. She remembered the look on her father's face, the direct, unwavering tone of his command, and the utter hopelessness that filled every fiber of her being as he'd introduced the lion with the dark, soulless eyes who sought to own her.

"Here she is." The smile on her father's face was forced and his tone held an undertone of steel, telling her not to argue but simply play along with whatever was said as he continued,

"King Reville, I am pleased to introduce my beautiful daughter, Scotlyn Olivia."

At the use of her full name, Scottie's eyes snapped to her father's. She shuddered at the rage simmering in their gunmetal grey depths, knowing it wasn't pointed at her but needing to ascertain what had caused such fury in the usually calm, cool, collected Leader of the largest Pride of mountain lions in North America. Cleander Cattanach had negotiated land disputes between warring nations, freed lions trapped by other Prides, Packs, and Clans, and even talked feuding Alphas out of fighting to the death without breaking a sweat, but never before had Scottie witnessed such utter wrath boiling inside of the man she called daddy. This was more than a simple meeting of Kings…something big was brewing, something that made Scottie's stomach do flips and her lioness issue a warning growl.

Trying the mental connection she'd shared with her father since birth, the Princess was shocked to find it blocked. Only once, the day of her mother's death while the great King was grieving, had he blocked the special bond they shared. Taking a deep breath, Scottie held tighter to the reins of her emotions and smiled sweetly as she held out her hand to King Reville.

Icy shards of dread slithered up her arm at the touch of Reville's hand, forcing her to hold back a shudder. Then he spoke, his smarmy voice exacerbating her anxiety as he leered, "Nice to meet you...again," showing his canines as he spoke and daring to wink at her like some randy teenager. "You've turned into quite a beautiful woman."

Although lions, as well as all shifters, could live for hundreds of years and aged very slowly, Scottie could see every year of Reville's age and knew he was eons her senior, which meant his flirting and winking made her skin crawl. She remembered how some had considered him handsome in his youth, a real catch. He was tall, muscular, and well-dressed. His thick, dark hair had just a touch of grey at the temples and had obviously been cut and styled by a professional.

Julia Mills

Scottie wasn't surprised to find his nails manicured or to see the huge onyx and gold signet ring he wore on his middle finger. Every King she'd met over the years wore them as a symbol of their station in life. The rings were always the same design, always gold but with a different colored stone to denote their Pride, all ostentatious and gaudy, and damn near as old as time, passed down from generation to generation of feline royalty. The old, puritanical, backward leaders of the feline shifter community used them as a way to announce to the world that they were 'King', well, all except her dad. Cleander's was locked in the safe hidden by the credenza behind his monstrous mahogany desk. He only took it out for special occasions or ceremonies where it held significance and had always joked that it was big and bulky and made him feel like a girl.

Noting the set of her father's shoulders and clenched fists at the other Leo's show of aggression, Scotlyn pulled herself from her musings as she tilted her head to the side, allowed her lioness to show in her eyes, and let the full force of her southern accent

32

loose when she answered, "It is indeed an unexpected pleasure to see you again, King Reville."

She wanted to laugh out loud at the thoughts and comments flying around the room from her father's Beta and Guards. Having known her for all of her life, the male lions knew exactly how pissed off she was and were actually having fun trying to decide what she'd do next.

Dilan's comment was her favorite, "Holy Lord, Scottie's channeling her southern belle. Hold onto your hats boys, we're either gonna get a cavity or go wading. It just depends on whether she lures him in with sugar or tries to baffle him with bullshit."

Biting her tongue, the Princess planned payback for her favorite 'uncle' and her dad's second in command as she pushed their teasing to the background and once again focused on the mountain lion before her, asking, "To what do we owe the honor of your visit, sir?" while expertly extricating her hand from Reville's and taking a big step backward.

The rise of the slimy lion's eyebrow said he had seen her step back but viewed it as a challenge. Scottie wanted to roll her eyes but refrained as she asked Piotr, the Pride's Tracker and a certifiable smartass, through their unique mental link, "Why do men think everything is a pissing contest? Is it in your DNA or just something you guys learn at birth?"

"A little of both," he chuckled, then his tone turned serious as he added, "but be careful with this one, deirfiúr beag, he's a right foul git."

"Great," was all she could say. Not only was Piotr being serious, which was unusual enough, but he sounded like Mel Gibson in Braveheart and had not taken his piercing blue eyes off the back of King Reville's head during their entire conversation – all things that had Scottie plotting her plans for escape while trying not to gag as Reville stepped closer and, with a smile that chilled her to the bone, replied, "Just a little unfinished business between your father and I." He leaned forward before adding,

"And, please call me, Basil...Scotlyn. We have, after all, known each other for years."

There was no doubt that the leader of the Reville Pride made her skin crawl, but there was more to it. She could read the old King like a book. He was conniving and underhanded, untrustworthy and vindictive, and worst of all, bloodthirsty. It was all in his eyes, obsidian windows that only magnified the depravity of not only the man, but also the mountain lion who dwelled within. His soul was barren, and if Scottie wasn't mistaken, the stupid son of a bitch wanted to drag both her and her father down with him.

The rest of the evening had been nothing short of torture. During dinner, the bastard left his mind wide open, letting every lascivious comment and vulgar insinuation flow directly at Scottie. Thankfully, Molly, the cook, spilled an entire bowl of bouillabaisse in Reville's lap, allowing the Princess to feign a headache and disappear. Unfortunately, that was not the last she would ever hear of Reville.

Later that night, after she'd listened to the sound of the bastard and his entourage finally leave, Cleander knocked on her door. "Come in," she called to her father as she turned off the TV.

Watching the usually stately King walk across the threshold with his head down and his shoulders slumped made all the red flags wave and the warning bells go off in Scottie's mind. Then he sat on the side of her bed, patted her legs and, without looking at her, used the nickname he hadn't called her since the day they spread her mother's ashes over the mountaintop.

"Kitten, I'm afraid I have some bad news." Cleander sighed. "I've tried everything I know, consulted every attorney, judge, and elected official both feline and human I can find, and the pact is airtight. There's no way to fight it, get out of it, or buy the son of a bitch off."

With each word her father spoke, Scottie's heart beat faster, sweat trickled down her spine, and her lioness restlessly paced the confines of her mind. Something really bad was about to happen. Something her father couldn't stop. Something that was going to affect the Princess in inconceivable ways for the rest of her very, very long life, and all she could do was sit...and wait...and pray.

The pendulum on the antique clock sitting on the mantel swung back and forth, the tick sounded like the banging of a gong as it echoed through the tense silence of her room. Scottie was afraid to breathe, afraid to think. She could only watch her father and hope that whatever he was about to tell her wasn't as bad as she imagined.

No longer able to stand the suspense, she reached for her father at the same time he looked up at her. Gasping, Scottie's hand hung in the air above Cleander's arm as she saw the unshed tears that filled his eyes.

"I am so sorry, Kitten." His voice cracked and a tear slid down his cheek. "But when my father extended our lands to the south, he made a pact with Basil's." Reaching up, Cleander took her hand in his, held it tight, and went on, "The Elder Reville was

37

even more of a bastard than his son, but on this one occasion, he readily agreed and deeded the land over to my father and our Pride for an extremely fair price."

Her father laid her hand on the bed, stood, and begin to pace as he continued talking, "But when your grandfather was reading the paperwork, he found that Old Reville had added a clause, stating that my first-born son would become a member of the Reville Pride upon his thirty-fifth birthday." He stopped at the window, ran his fingers through his already disheveled red hair, and shook his head. "According to Dilan, my father fought the bastard tooth and nail but, in the end, he had to give in and agree to the deal. We needed the access to the water, not to mention, some of our people had already been allowed to set up housekeeping on the newly acquired territory."

Cleander paused and Scottie took the opportunity to ask, "But why didn't Uncle Dilan ever tell you and what does that have to do with me?"

Turning slowly, her father put his hands in his pockets as he shrugged, "Dilan was sworn to secrecy. He was dad's Beta before he was mine. It was his duty to keep his secrets, just as he keeps mine." Her dad smiled a sad smile. "Then you were born a Princess instead of a Prince and before we could have another child, your mother fell ill, so he and your grandfather figured there was no need to alarm anyone. What was done was done, Fate had decided to bless us with you and the pact was null and void."

His words hung in the air as he let his chin drop to his chest and blew out a long-suffering breath. When he looked up again, rage had replaced his sadness in the deep green eyes of his lion. "However, Basil found a loophole," Cleander growled through gritted teeth. "An old clause in one of the bylaws of the Pride Council's Feline Assembly and he has received a favorable ruling from the High Court."

The stinging scent of her father's fury bit at her senses, fear caused her blood to run cold, her lioness' roar echoed through her mind, and all Scottie could do was shake her head and whisper, "No…please…no…" until the words she'd most feared fell from her father's mouth.

"The court has ruled that you and Basil are to be mated on the next full moon."

Mumbled sounds coming from Marrok thankfully pulled Scottie from her memories. What was it about the handsome Alpha that made her heart beat faster and her lioness purr? She'd known him for years, watched him step into his father's shoes at a young age, raise his sister and become a formidable leader of one of the largest Wolf Packs in the States, not to mention turn the heads of every woman who came within a hundred yards. But now, it was as if she was seeing him for the first time and Goddess help her, she really, really *liked* what she saw.

Chapter Three

Rolling towards the wonderfully tender touch of the woman from

 his dream, Marrok slowly changed from wolf to man as he put off opening his eyes for as long as possible. Stretching his arms over his head, the Alpha inhaled deeply, filling

his lungs with the succulent scent of citrus and woman. Smiling

to himself, he had just decided to sink back into the wonderful

abyss of his reverie when a lyrically low contralto caused his eyes

to spring open and his wolf to sit up and take notice.

"Now, open those pretty eyes for me, big guy."

Sitting straight up, shocked to find the hands he had felt

so lovingly petting his fur were real and more than that, attached

to an absolutely gorgeous female, Marrok grabbed her hands

where they still touched his stomach and asked with more

suspicion than he'd intended, "Scottie? What the hell are *you*

doing here?"

Grinning like the cat that ate the canary, Scotlyn Cattanach, the daughter of the King of the neighboring mountain lion Pride, tilted her head to the side, flashed her gorgeous green eyes at him, and purred, "Just a little bit of trespassing." Her smile widened as she gently pulled her hands from his and held them up with her wrists together. "Wanna tie me up and interrogate me for my crimes, *big guy*?"

Caught in the snare of her beauty and her playful nature, along with a myriad of feelings and emotions he'd never felt before, Marrok gently wrapped his fingers around Scotlyn's upper arms, pulled her into his lap, and crushed his lips to hers. Fire raced through his veins, his wolf howled long and loud in his mind, and need unlike any he'd ever known filled every fiber of his being, driving him to claim Scotlyn as his own.

His hands slid under the soft cotton of her blouse. Electricity shot from his fingertips, igniting every sense as he touched and teased the silken skin of her back. Scotlyn moaned into their kiss and her hips rolled against his as his hands slid from back to front. Dancing along the underside of her breasts, he teased her already hardened nipples through the soft fabric, his excitement growing stronger, more explosive by the second.

Craving more, *hungry* for every part of the lioness writhing in his arms, Marrok tore his lips from hers, pushed the blouse over her head, and laid Scotlyn on the cool grass, following her down as if she were the magnet and he the steel. Her hands dove into his hair, her nails scratching his scalp as she met him halfway with a kiss just as furious and frenzied as their first.

Arousal thickened in his blood. His erection grew harder still as he laid his body flush onto hers. Rolling his hips, cursing the clothes still separating them, Marrok reached between them and, in a matter of seconds, stripped not only his beautiful lioness but also himself, blessedly bare.

Scotlyn's nails, longer and sharper the more she lost control, scored his back as the tip of his cock slid along the inside of her thigh. Tearing her lips from his, her emerald cat eyes looked deep into his as she purred, "You are so much better than in my dreams."

Rolling his hips, he pushed through her already wet curls and teased the opening of her pussy as he responded, "Hold on, my little kitten, you ain't seen nothing yet."

Her nails dug into his ass. Liquid fire ran through his veins. The need to be inside Scotlyn, to have her, to mark her, became more than he could withstand. Kissing across her jaw, nibbling down her throat, he couldn't get enough of her scent, her taste...of *her*.

Looking down her body, he felt her eyes on him, but there was no looking away from the amazing feast before him. Kissing across her décolletage, moving down between her beautifully full breasts, Marrok hungrily sucked her nipple into his mouth. Teasing and taunting the hardened bit of flesh, his wolf growled in excitement as Scotlyn thrashed under the Alpha's muscled frame, begging, "Please, Marrok, please don't make me wait any longer."

Her nails, now claws, gripped his buttocks tighter as her hips thrust against his in an attempt to force their bodies together. Scotlyn's mind, awash with a desire that only he could quench, was completely opened to Marrok's. He felt what she felt, saw what she saw, and read her thoughts as if they were his own.

Moving from one breast to the other, he showed it the same attention. In her excitement, his lioness lifted her back off the ground, shoving her heated flesh farther into his mouth. He could feel how every lick, every nip of his teeth caused a jolt in her clit and made her pussy grasp at nothing with ferocious desire.

Need, lust, a hunger that shocked and thrilled his Scotlyn made her frenzied as she moaned, "Oh, my dear goddess, Marrok, yes...yes."

Her fingers wound through his hair. The scent of her arousal, warm citrus blossoms blooming in the sun and hot, wanton female, filled his senses. He needed to taste her, needed to have her essence coating his tongue, had to have a part of her inside him.

Scotlyn's eyes snapped opened as he slid down her body. She shook her head and pulled at his hair. "No, Marrok, I *need* you."

"And you shall have me," he winked, his voice low and rumbling and his brogue more pronounced even to his own ears.

Ignoring her continued protests and the pulls to his hair that made him think he might soon have bald spots, Marrok spread her thighs wide, placed her legs over his shoulders, and growled, "Mine," at the sight of her glistening red curls.

Anticipation simmered between them as he inhaled her scent, nearly drunk on the amazing aroma. Blowing on her aroused clit as its swollen tip peeked from amid her curls, Scotlyn's hips shot from the ground as she growled, "Now, oh my Goddess, Marrok, please. Are you trying to kill me?"

Her hips rose higher still, her strangled cry of "Marrok…" turning to a low moan of pleasure as he licked a tight circle around her clit.

No longer able to hold back, Marrok licked her pussy and sucked her clit, swallowing her juices as if they were manna from heaven. Scotlyn pushed against his face, forcing a growl from his lips. Her response was explosive, causing him to growl again as he drove his tongue ever deeper into her.

A wave of desire like a tsunami rolled through Scotlyn and in turn, through the Alpha. Her heels dug into his back. Her fingers tugged at his hair. Her screams filled the swamps as she was hurtled headlong into her orgasm.

Needing to be inside her, to feel her around him, Marrok moved with preternatural speed as he got to his knees and turned Scotlyn onto her stomach. Positioning his lioness on her hands and knees as she fought to catch her breath, he ran his hands down her silken back.

Scotlyn, looking over her shoulder, snared him with a look of pure lust. Her eyes aglow with her cat, his sexy lioness grinned. "Like what you see?"

"Very much." He kissed the small of her back, letting just the tip of his tongue tease the tender skin then looked up, thrilled to see her eyes now half-lidded and her lips open in a pant. "And I intend to make it mine."

He felt the fur of his wolf push through the skin along his jaw, saw it on the backs of his hand as his nails elongated.

"Then make me yours."

Something broke within him at the sound of Scotlyn's sassy retort. Marrok leaned forward, caging her in. He licked down her spine, loving her shiver and the goose bumps on her glistening skin. Once again paying special attention to the small of her back, the Alpha grabbed his mate's hips as he slipped the head of his cock into her sleek channel.

"Oh, my Goddess, yes...yes..." Scotlyn moaned, her head falling forward as her hips pushed back against him.

He couldn't stop. The Hunger was too great. He needed to be inside her, needed to be one with his mate, needed to mark her from the inside-out. Entering Scotlyn in one smooth glide, the air rushed from his lungs as he felt her pussy stretching around him. Plastering his chest to her back, he kissed the nape of her neck while rolling his hips ever so slightly, letting her get used to his size.

"Marrok, *please*..."

No sooner had Scotlyn uttered the words than Marrok quickly pulled back, thrusting back in even faster. Fire rushed through his veins. He felt the answering call within his lioness. Driven by desire, he thrust over and over as his mate met him stroke for stroke.

He felt her body tighten, knew she was once again on the edge of pleasure. Lust, all-encompassing desire, and *Hunger* ate at the Alpha and his beast. Hard and fast he thrust in and out of his mate as she pleaded, "Marrok...please..."

"Yes, Scotlyn." He panted then growled as his claws dug into her hips, *"Mine."*

Her head once again fell forward. Her red curls danced among the blades of grass beside where her claws dug into the earth. Scotlyn panted, her pussy contracted around him, pushing his arousal higher, driving him out of his mind.

"Say it!" Marrok snarled. "Mine! You. Are. Mine."

Her pussy tightened around him. Her head raised and her hair flew over her shoulder as she turned her head and looked back at him as she panted, "Yes, Marrok. I am yours."

At the sound of her admission, Marrok lost all control. Fur sprouted along his arms and legs. He could feel it outlining his spine and covering his shoulders as he claimed his mate the way nature had intended...hard, deep, and rough.

Scotlyn begged him to continue. He saw the fur of her lioness pushing through her skin. Listened to the rough sounds of her pleasure as her teeth grew. One final slap of her hips against his and his mate was flying. Her pussy gripped his cock like a vice. Her essence flowed freely, wetting the back of her thighs and the front of his.

He watched the fireworks exploding in her mind, knew the moment her climax was at a peak and then, at precisely the pinnacle of her orgasm, Marrok bit her. He watched the erotic tension inside her, the desire that they had built together, shatter into a million pieces as her roar of pleasure echoed through the swamp.

The feel of his teeth sinking into her shoulder, the warm taste of her blood flowing across his tongue and the joy he felt filling his mate's body was the most incredible sensation the Alpha had ever experienced.

Answering her roar, Marrok bellowed, "Mine!"

Scotlyn was still quaking with mini orgasms as Marrok drove into her one final time. His cock thickened and, from one second to the next, he came in quick short bursts. Her pussy sucked him ever deeper as he bathed her insides with his warm essence.

Slowly regaining his wits, Marrok slid from Scotlyn and gently rolled them over, laying her across his chest while she still struggled to catch her breath. Running his hands down her back, the Alpha chuckled as she shivered, opened one eye, and sighed, "Damn, Marrok, where have you been all my life?"

Raising his head, he held his lips to hers and whispered, "Right here, my little kitten, right here."

Chapter Four

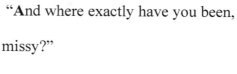

"**And** where exactly have you been, missy?"

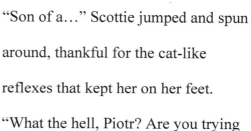

"Son of a…" Scottie jumped and spun around, thankful for the cat-like reflexes that kept her on her feet.

"What the hell, Piotr? Are you trying

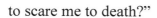

to scare me to death?"

Sauntering forward with his usual shit-eating grin plastered on his face, the Tracker and all-around pain-in-the-ass but a good guy nonetheless, chuckled. "Nope, just taking advantage of you sneaking in during the wee hours of the morning for the first time in ages." He leaned against the fence, wiping his hands on a holey rag. "Reliving your glory days?" The mountain lion winked and pushed his Stetson back on his head. "Or creatin' all new ones?"

Rolling her eyes, sure to keep turned to the side so Piotr couldn't see Marrok's mark on her neck, Scottie feigned irritation and sighed, "I was just running the swamp."

It was all she could do not to smile and touch the spot where the Alpha wolf's bite still tingled. Never had she imagined finding a mate, let alone her True Mate, the one designed by the Goddess just for her, but there was no denying what had happened between them. Now, to escape prying eyes so she could think. It was going to take a miracle, along with some seriously fast talking, to get out of the mess with Basil.

Taking a step towards the house, Scottie stopped and looked over her shoulder when Piotr's tone turned sad as he asked, "How long?"

"How long what?" she asked, still thinking of Marrok and what they had shared.

Closing the distance between them, the Tracker asked, "How long until you have to go to Basil?"

"Oh. That." She looked at the ground. "Well, the full moon is eight days away, so a week." Pain shot through her chest at the thought of leaving the swamp, leaving her home and most of all, leaving Marrok. With unwanted tears filling her eyes, Scottie threw back her shoulders and straightened her spine. "So, we've got seven days to raise hell. You in?"

Forcing a smile, Piotr nodded and snickered, "Whatever you say, Princess."

"Then you get the crew together. Let's get this party started *tonight*. Say, ten 'o'clock?"

His shit-eating grin was back as she felt Piotr forcing his sadness away. Nodding, he added, "If you've got the beer, you know I've got the time. And the boys were born ready."

"Good. Let's meet at the house." She started walking away and then added, "Now, don't be late," over her shoulder.

"Never," Piotr laughed out loud.

Noting that her father's pickup was blessedly absent from its usual parking space, Scottie went through the kitchen, said hello to Molly and Shef, another of her father's Betas. As she grabbed a muffin and a cup of coffee before running up the back stairs to her room. With her hand on the knob of the door to her room, the lioness thought she'd gotten away with her night out when Dilan's voice stopped her dead in her tracks.

"Just getting home?" her father's second-in-command and the man she'd called uncle her whole life asked.

Going with her usual sarcasm and more than a little attitude, Scottie turned her head, strategically hiding her love bite, raised an eyebrow, and asked, "Is that breaking news around here? Piotr asked me the same thing." She sighed. "Y'all need to get a life. There has got to be something more interesting than my comings and goings."

"Scotlyn…" Dilan gave a warning growl.

"Uncle Dilan…" Scottie grumbled in response, bursting out laughing when the Beta failed to hide his smile at her sass.

Regaining his composure, the mountain lion schooled his expression. "Your father would lose his mind if he knew you were out all night."

"Well, I guess we just can't tell him then, right?" Immediately angry at the situation and what she was facing because of some stupid debt, Scottie narrowed her eyes and in a flippant tone added, "It's a good thing I'll be gone soon. Outta sight, outta mind."

"Now, Scotlyn, you know…"

"I know nothing, Dilan, but that I am being forced to marry an evil son-of-a-bitch." She pushed open her door with such force it banged against the wall as she went on, "So if I want to dance naked on tables and fuck everything between here and Orlando for the next seven days, there's not a damn thing you *or* Daddy can do about it."

Stepping across the threshold of her room, she grabbed the side of the door and flung it shut with a loud bang then yelled, "And you can tell him I said so."

She knew it wasn't her father's fault or Dilan's or anyone's but the Grand Poobah of all bastards, Basil Reville, that she was being forced to repay their old family debt. The son of a whore had found a way to twist the law to fit his whims. Scottie should've seen it coming. Had been fending off the old lion's advances since her eighteenth birthday. He was lecherous scum and should have been neutered and put out to pasture years ago.

"Boy, I would love to wield that scalpel." Scottie chuckled out loud as she grabbed her favorite terry robe and fluffy towel and headed to the bathroom for a shower.

Goosebumps covered her arms and legs as the warm water flowed over her body reminding her of the magic in Marrok's touch and the incredible attraction she felt for the Alpha. Visions of what they had shared floated through her mind. It was more than the act of having sex or even making love, it was the soul deep connection that they shared, the way their minds, bodies, and hearts became one. The unexplainable, magical way they had shared one another's feelings. Leaving him lying in the grass after he'd marked her as his own was one of the hardest things Scottie had ever had to do. She knew beyond all doubt there would never be another man for her; Marrok was the one and only. Family debts, deals made, bastards trying to take her homelands…none of it mattered. She had to find a way to get out of mating Basil or die trying.

"And they said I didn't have a flair for the dramatic in school. I would've been one hell of a Juliet, tragic love and all," she sighed, washing the conditioner out of her hair as images of Marrok's passion-filled eyes, the deep green of the lily pads that covered her favorite pool in the swamp, floated through her mind.

Her body ached to once again be with her Alpha, to hear the beat of his heart in sync with hers and inhale the wonderfully fresh scent of man, wolf, and mate. Never had she slept so soundly, felt so safe or protected as she had by Wolf's Lake in the arms of the man who inextricably owned her, body and soul.

Wrapping her hair in a towel and donning her pink fluffy robe, Scottie laid down on her bed, promising herself it was for just a few minutes as she immediately fell asleep. Dreams of a happily ever after with Marrok was interrupted by a loud pounding on her door and a chuckled, "Wake up Sleeping Beauty, we've all been waiting by the Escalade for nearly a half hour."

"Piotr?" Scottie asked, stifling a yawn and pulling the towel still wrapped around her hair from her head. "What the hell? What time is it?"

"Ten-thirty. Can I come in or would you prefer I keep yelling so all your dad's friends can hear?"

"Get your ass in here," she snickered, climbing off the bed and looking at the clock.

"Wow, you'll be the belle of the ball looking like that."

"Shut. Up." Scottie feigned irritation before chuckling. "I can't believe I slept the whole day away." She entered the bathroom and looked in the mirror, trying to decide what to do with the tangled mess of red curls atop her head.

"You're not as young as you used to be. Late nights are hard for you old gals." Piotr fell back on Scottie's bed, narrowly missing the hair brush she threw at him.

"Because you are *so* much younger than me." The lioness sprayed detangler in her hair and grabbed another brush. "What is it, five days?"

"Six and almost twelve hours, thank you very much."

Laughing out loud, Scottie abandoned trying to style her hair and instead, piled it on top of her head in a messy bun, let some curls frame her face then turned to the man she considered her adopted brother and asked, "Look okay?"

"Looks okay to me, but then again, what do I know?"

Rolling her eyes again, Scottie put her hand on her hip and sassed, "Thanks, I feel so much better now."

Throwing his hands out in front of him in mock surrender, Piotr smiled his most charming smile, complete with a twinkle in his crystal blue eyes and the dimple in his left cheek shining, and gave the lioness a quick wink while nodding. "Give me a break, you're pretty even when you're covered in mud and cursing like a sailor and you know it. Now, hurry your ass up or I'm leavin' ya' here."

Grinning from ear-to-ear, Scottie thanked the lion, walked into her closet, shut the door, and quickly got dressed in her favorite black jeans, red scoop neck tee, and boots. She barely had the door open before Piotr was once again complaining, "Ten-forty-five, come on Scots. I'm dying here. My beer tank is low. I'm in danger of thirsting to death as slow as you are."

"Hold your damn horses. I need a little mascara, blush, and lip gloss."

"Oh, my Goddess, woman. You're killin' me here."

"Okay, okay, first rounds on me. Just hush."

"First three rounds, more like it."

"Two and don't push your luck," Scottie growled, grabbing her mascara and coating her light red lashes with the black liquid. Two quick swipes of blush on each cheek, some peach gloss on her lips, and a last look in the mirror had the lioness out of the bathroom, grabbing her bag, and calling over her shoulder, "Come on, slowpoke. I thought you were in a hurry."

"I'm right behind ya', Princess." Piotr chuckled as he followed her to the right and down the back stairs. "Are you avoiding the old man?"

"You know it. I want to have fun and forget about all this BS for a few hours."

"I hear ya'. I'm also guessing he hasn't seen that massive mark on your neck."

Stopping dead in her tracks, Scottie slapped her hand over the proof of Marrok's bite, spun on her toes, smashed her purse into Piotr's chest, and ran back up the stairs, calling over her shoulder, "Go get everyone into the SUV. I'll be right back." Then quickly added, "And you could've said something before."

"Yeah, but what fun would that have been?" Piotr barked with laughter.

"I really hate you sometimes," Scottie grumbled under her breath as she swung open the door to her bedroom.

"You love me, and you know it," came Piotr's snickered response a split second before she heard the back door open and the sound of the heels of his boots on the wooden steps leading to the garage.

Grabbing a thick black satin choker with a cat's eye stone set in platinum, Scottie quickly secured the clasp, made sure the fabric covered the miraculous mark on her neck and ran back down the stairs to join the others. Ignoring Piotr's stifled chuckle and shit-eating grin, the lioness plastered on a smile and yelled, "Come on, y'all. First two rounds are on me."

"Hell yeah," was the general consensus from the four men she'd known her whole life as they climbed into the white Escalade.

The trip to their favorite bar, The Shift, owned by a family of grizzly bear shifters who had lived on Pride lands since before Scottie's grandfather was born, took less than twenty minutes. It was a short but lively ride, during which time, the Princess and her adopted brothers argued over what radio station they would listen to and made bets over who would get hit on first.

Of course, the lioness was sure it would be Piotr with his big blue eyes, wavy blonde hair that defied being tamed, and his quick-witted charm, but she would never tell the others. Hell, they were all gorgeous. She'd watched women literally trip over their own two feet while staring at the group of mountain lion shifters. It was still a mystery to her why they were all still single or at the very least, didn't date. They were her surrogate brothers, the best of their Pride, and Scottie wanted to see them happy.

Country music shattered the stillness of the night as Sampson, the youngest lion of the group by twelve minutes, opened the heavy oak door of the bar. Scottie mussed his collar-length brown curls as she walked past him, whispering, "Thanks, kiddo. Now, get in here and win that bet."

Josiah, Sampson's identical twin and older by those same twelve minutes, tapped Scottie on the shoulder and pointed at a table to the right of the dance floor while she followed the rest of her crew to the bar. Teddy, the oldest son and next to inherit the bar, winked at her and asked, "What'll y'all have?"

Scottie loved his low, deep growly voice and the fact that he was the fifth Teddy in a family of grizzlies, not that she would ever, *ever* call the seven-foot-four-inch muscled giant *Teddy Bear* to his face. "Five shots of Patron and a bucket of silver bullets."

"You got it, Scottie," Teddy nodded. "I'll have Sylvia bring it over."

Sylvia was the first girl to be born to the MacBhaird Sloth in over a century. To say the males all kept a close eye on her was an understatement. The Cattanach Betas were among the few males allowed to talk to her without one of her brothers or worse yet, her father, by her side.

"Thanks, Teddy," she grinned. "Don't forget you owe me a dance."

"You got it, Scots."

Making her way to the table, Scottie wasn't surprised to see that damn near every female eye in the place was on her Pride mates. Deciding to see what trouble she could stir up, the lioness pulled Hammond, the quietest but most striking of the Betas with short black hair and shoulders for days, onto the dance floor. His whiskey-colored eyes narrowed suspiciously as he asked, "What are you up to?"

"Nothing. Why?" she teased. "Can't I give you a leg up in winning the bet? I would love to see you take two-hundred dollars from those loud mouths."

Smiling and nodding, the lion quickly agreed and together, the couple danced until they were out of breath and a line of women waiting to cut-in had literally behind them. Patting Hammond on the shoulder, Scottie winked, "Looks like you're the winner." Then added in a low murmur that had the mountain lion laughing out loud, "In more ways than one."

Turning towards the bar, sure one of her crew had downed her shot along with all the beer at least two songs ago, Scottie nearly tripped over her own two feet as her senses filled with the scent of fresh air and Alpha wolf. Jerking her head to the left, the lioness didn't even try to stop her smile when her eyes met his.

Marrok's low rumbling voice filled her mind, making her body tingle and her heart race. *"Of all the gin joints in all the world, thank God you walked into mine."*

Chapter Five

After returning home as the sun was rising over the Cypress trees,

 Marrok locked himself in his office and attempted to work on the wording of the treaty with the Blue Ridge Pack. Restless and exponentially more irritable than

he'd been since waking up to find Scotlyn gone, he read Olivia's

notes and growled about the other Pack's whining for more

benefits. Shuffling the stack of papers that comprised the legal

pact to the list of provisions, he read them again, making it about

halfway through before slamming his free hand onto the hard oak

surface of his desk and flinging the sheets into the air, watching

as they floated to the floor like large white butterflies. It didn't

matter what he read or how long he stared at the pages, all he saw

was Scotlyn's beautiful face.

After shattering his favorite coffee mug with his bare

hands, Marrok jumped to his feet and alternated between pacing the floor and staring out the window in the direction of the huge two-story brick home of his lioness. Of course, that only led to more frustration, more visions of *her.* and an insatiable need to be by her side, which at that moment was just not possible.

Bursting out of the Grande Hall, Marrok stomped to his house, snarling at nearly anyone who had the courage to speak to him, then slammed the door so hard upon entering that the pictures bounced against the walls. He needed to think, needed to come up with a way to make the crotchety, old mountain lion King accept a wolf as the mate of his daughter. Marrok had known Cleander Cattanach, as well as every other lion in his Pride, for his entire life. They were purists in the most extreme sense of the word. They would be friends with almost anyone, share their land with other species they trusted, even drink a beer or two with non-felines, but never, *ever* would they mate outside the feline family.

Marrok recalled several disputes that ended in fights to the death when other-natured shifters had sniffed too close to a feline female. He would do whatever it took to be with Scotlyn. She was his Destiny, the Fated mate promised to him by the Goddess herself, and nothing and no one, not even Cleander Cattanach, was going to stop him. The Alpha just hoped it didn't come to a fight to the death with the King. It was definitely *not* how he wanted to start his forever with the Princess.

Snatching his cell phone off the counter as the irritating tone Olivia had changed it too filled his kitchen, Marrok snarled, "What?"

"Nice to talk to you too, Chief. I guess I don't need to ask how you're feeling today."

Hanging his head and taking a deep breath, Marrok tried to sound civil when he answered, "Sorry, Finn. It's just…well, I don't…I mean…"

"You mean that lioness has got ya' all tied up in your BVDs and you're seeing double trying not to snatch her from her daddy's house and hightail it outta the swamp." Marrok's Beta chuckled. "'Bout sum it up?"

"Yes, dammit…and…"

"And now that you've spent the night with her, the Hunger is about to eat you alive but you have to figure out a way to convince ol' Cleander that you're her man, or wolf, as the case may be."

Shaking his head and smiling despite the pure unadulterated desire clawing at his insides, Marrok snorted, "So, have you been reading my mind, eavesdropping, or snooping?"

"None of the above, my friend, I just happen to have seen you tearing a path through the courtyard and knew what was up. Well, that and I saw you sneaking in at sunup. Although, I will say that you need to secure your mental blocks a little tighter unless you're planning to share your dilemma with the whole Pack. I don't mind ignoring your broadcasts, but I'm thinking there's a few old busybodies around here who might have a lot of fun with the pictures floating around your noggin at the moment."

"Son of a bitch!" The Alpha ground out through gritted teeth as he swiped his hand across the breakfast bar, throwing his mail, newspapers, and the wolf salt and pepper shaker Olivia had given him as a gag gift all over the floor.

"Whoa, whoa, whoa, hold on there, Hoss, it's not that bad."

"Not that bad? Not that bad?!" Marrok roared. "I feel like something is trying to crawl its way out of my brain. I go from angry to horny and back to angry like I'm spinning around in a revolving door and now you tell me I'm broadcasting my X-rated thoughts about the Princess of the neighboring Pride to everyone in my Pack!" The Alpha panted through gritted teeth like he'd just run twenty miles in the August sun before growling, "Would you like to tell me exactly what could be worse?"

His question was met with utter silence, which lasted approximately three seconds before his best friend, Beta, and all around good guy burst out laughing. "You could have been caught streaking through the Memorial Garden naked, but then you've done that before."

Throwing his phone across the room, Marrok stood staring at pieces of metal and plastic laying on the tile floor for almost a full minute before there was a knock at his door. "Come in, asshole," he bellowed, not even turning around when the door opened and Finn chuckled. "Good thing I keep a drawer full of replacement phones in my office."

The grey and black wolf strode into the kitchen, turned one of the chairs around, and straddled the seat before placing his arms across its high-runged back. Shaking his head, he smirked, "What you need is a night out to clear your head and get a new perspective on things."

"Yeah, and kill everyone in my path." Marrok ran his fingers through his hair before making his way to the fridge, grabbing a bottle of water, and throwing one at Finn. After drinking it down in one gulp, the Alpha stalked out to the family room, paced along the floor-to-ceiling windows that covered one entire wall, and looked out into the swamp, praying for an easy fix to what ailed him.

"You won't kill anyone," Finn sighed. "I'll be there." Marrok heard the Beta's chair scrape the floor then his footsteps on the tile before he walked up beside him and added, "Besides, what's the worst thing that could happen? Teddy and his brothers throw us out?" The grey and black wolf slapped Marrok on the shoulder, barking with laughter. "Won't be the first time and I know as sure as God made little green apples, it won't be the last."

"I just don't know. I'm not in control, Finn." He ran his hands through his tangled hair for the umpteenth time that day and blew out a long breath. "This is worse than my first change, my first full moon, and my first case of bloodlust all wrapped into one." He looked his Beta in the eye and grabbed him by the shoulders. "I feel like I'm losing my fucking mind here. What if…"

"What if nothing." Marrok could feel his Beta pushing healing power and control through the link they shared as Packmates and best friends as he spoke. "I got you. I won't let anything happen." The grey and black wolf patted the Alpha on the shoulder before taking a step back. "But I understand your worry. Remember, I've seen you in action and had to deliver the new chairs and pool table to The Shift after you and that stupid coyote decided to see who was the real Alpha."

Marrok smiled at the memory, thinking that busting a few heads might just make him feel better. Then he saw Scotlyn's face, heard her low, soft voice in his mind, and knew that fighting was not the answer.

Turning back to the window, the Alpha listened as his Beta continued, "I'll do ya' one better than me. I'll see if Errol and Thane can go with us. They've been itching to get off guard duty and we never properly celebrated them rising to Beta status."

The Alpha was somehow sure he was making a mistake but also knew there was no way he could stay cooped up all night without tearing his house down or worse, sitting outside Scotlyn's window like a lovesick pup, so he reluctantly agreed. "Do it. Make the call. I'm going to make something to eat and shower."

"I've got a better idea." Finn winked with a wicked glint in his eye. "I know just what you need to take the edge off. How about a run and a little hunt? Meat on the bone always makes you feel better and we can go way out to the west swamp. It's deserted and with any luck, you'll get to wrestle a gator."

So, that was what they did. Finn had been right, by the time they got back to Marrok's house, he'd taken a bit of the bite out of the Hunger and could at least focus on showering and getting ready. They met the younger Betas just outside the Grande Hall and all together, the wolves made their way to The Shift.

Stepping out of the truck, Marrok's boot had barely touched the asphalt when he was nearly bowled over by a fiery wave of desire and insatiable need that filled him from the inside-out and threatened to reduce both man and wolf to ash. Leaning against the hood of his truck, the Alpha hung his head and panted until his vision cleared and he could make out what his Packmates were asking.

"You okay?" Thane asked.

"What the hell?" Errol sounded worried.

"Thane, go get him some water," Finn ordered.

Shaking his head, Marrok stammered, "N-n-no, I'm good. Just give me a sec to catch my breath. Y'all go on in. I'll be right behind you."

It wasn't until his Betas opened the door and the sound of her laughter reached his ears that Marrok knew the reason he was once again in the full-on thrall of the Hunger. Making a beeline into the club, the Alpha could only stare as he watched the tantalizing sway of Scotlyn's hips as she made her way to the bar. Captivated by the woman who already owned him body and soul, the Alpha's mind reached for hers, chuckling at her quick-witted response to his movie reference quip.

"Looks more like you walked into mine, you long, tall drink of just what I was thirsty for."

Looking into her eyes, Marrok knew there was no way he would last much longer without having her in his arms. *"Meet me out back."*

"I like the way you think." Scotlyn's chuckled reply made his cock jump and his wolf howl. *"You go out the front door, I'll sneak out the side."* She winked. *"Last one there is a silly wolf."*

No sooner were the words floating through his mind than his mate was making her way towards the side door. Turning on his heels, ignoring Finn's calls from the bar, Marrok pushed through the huge double doors, made a quick left, and ran to the back of the building.

Racing around the corner, he gained speed at the sight of his miraculous mate, slowing only when she was in his arms and his lips were on hers. Their kiss was ravenous. Her hands were immediately in his hair, holding him to her as she opened completely. Lifting her off the ground, Marrok grabbed the full globes of her ass, backing her against the stone wall of the bar as he ground his hips against hers, cursing the clothing that separated them.

Marrok kissed across her jaw and nibbled down her neck, unable to get enough of the lovely creature Fate had seen fit to create just for him. Scotlyn's legs wrapped around his waist as she ground her hips against his, gasping, "Oh, Marrok, yes, oh my Goddess. I missed you so much."

Her hands pulled at his hair and grabbed at his shoulders as he tore the satin ribbon from her neck and teased his mark with his teeth and tongue. Scotlyn's leg closed tighter around him, pulling him closer, holding him tight. Bending his knees, changing his position ever so slightly, Marrok thrust his denim-covered erection against his lioness' center and smiled against her skin as she growled his name and her nails, now claws, bit into his skin.

Raising his head, he commanded, his voice now more beast than man, "Look at me, Scotlyn."

Her eyes snapped open, their lovely emerald green shining in the darkness. Her pupils now elliptical as the lioness of her soul also looked at him. "You are mine," he growled, smashing his lips to hers and adding, *"Now, and forever, mine,"* directly into her mind.

"Yes! Yes, Marrok! Yours!" Her affirmation filled his mind a split second before a sharp pain, like that of a large hypodermic needle, struck the thick muscle in the back of his left thigh.

Tearing his lips from Scotlyn's, the Alpha roared in pain as fire raced through his veins and his vision blurred. Pain wracked his body. His muscles went limp. It was all Marrok could do to keep his mate from hitting the asphalt as he fell to his knees. A roar, angry and threatening, sprang from Scotlyn's lips even as her image warped and wiggled, going in and out of focus as Marrok's ass hit the ground.

"Marrok, get…" Was all he could make out as his mate tried to pull him to his feet seconds before she once again roared then jumped to protect him from the thundering footsteps pounding towards them.

Falling onto his back, the Alpha rolled to his side. He could hear Scotlyn threatening someone, but it sounded as if she were a million miles away.

"Get back!" she shouted. "I'll tear you limb from limb."

Then came a scuffle. The sound of fists hitting flesh accompanied by a very male grunt and then Scotlyn's roar that ended with a loud "Oomph," followed by hurried footsteps.

No longer able to see, Marrok reached into the darkness, calling for his mate, struggling to get up, "Scotlyn! Scotlyn!"

Marrok

His wolf roared in his head just as an unfamiliar male voice chastised, "The boss said not to hurt her." Which was quickly answered by, "She's not hurt, just unconscious, and no longer using your face for a punching bag."

Thank God, she got a few punches in...

No longer able to speak, his consciousness quickly draining away, Marrok mentally called to Finn, *"Find Scotlyn."*

Chapter Six

Struggling to open her eyes seemed like way too much trouble,

 especially since she already knew who had kidnapped her and had a general idea where she was being held. No matter where she smelled, her senses were filled with the acrid scent of Basil's old cat smell, nasty cologne, and his utter desperation.

That sorry son of a bitch doesn't know what desperation is. Just wait until I get my claws into his mangy ass...

Keeping her breathing slow and deep, Scottie had been playing possum since her butt hit the lumpy cot. She listened to the stupid mountain lions boast about how they'd bested the biggest Alpha wolf in the state. The longer they told the story, the bigger they said Marrok was and exaggerated how fast he'd hit the ground. It was like the fish tale but with a wolf and a dart gun. More than once, she'd thought about jumping up and telling them what freakin' cowards they were for hiding behind a stinky

dumpster to hide their scents, shooting her wolf with a dart from

at least two yards away, and then running in to grab her only

when the Alpha was down for the count. But it wasn't worth

wasting her breath.

*Your day will come, asshats. And I will be the one telling
stories...*

Used to being in control, the one in charge, Scotty was

about to go batty laying like a lump on a stinky cot. She couldn't

smell much but Basil's scent because of the chloroform still

burning her nose. She couldn't move because of the silver cuffs

on her wrists and ankles. She couldn't speak telepathically

because of the dirty magic stinging her skin and worst of all, she

had to pee.

Worse. Date. Ever.

Although it really hadn't been a date, had it? She'd been

dancing away the night, trying to think of anything other than

Marrok and in walked her long tall Alpha mate. He looked better than homemade sin and tasted twice as good.

She loved his shoulder-length auburn hair that refused to be tamed, the soft glow of his dark green eyes, his easy smile, and the wide set of his shoulders. If she was honest, there was nothing she *didn't* like about her mate. But what turned her inside-out, upside-down and made both woman and lioness sit up and take notice was the way he made her feel with just one glance. It was earth-shattering, life-affirming, and something she refused to live without. To hell with family debts, obligations, and most of all, to hell with Basil Fucking Reville. Scottie would see the sorry son of a…

The sound of approaching footsteps combined with a snicker cut off Scottie's thoughts and had her turning her head towards the voice.

"You might as well open your eyes, Scotlyn, I can tell you're awake."

Glaring, praying that daggers would shoot from her eyes and spear the bastard through the heart, Scottie refused to answer Basil as he stood before her with a smug expression and posing like it was a photo op. Stepping forward, he knelt beside the cot and smirked, "If you behave yourself, I'll let the boys take those nasty silver shackles off and you can sit up. I see no reason why we can't be civilized while discussing the future." He reached forward and brushed the hair off her forehead, making the nachos she'd had earlier in the evening threaten to make an abrupt reappearance.

Moving her head as far back as she could, the lioness continued to stare as she ground out, "Just get on with whatever you're planning. I neither want nor need your civility."

"Now, now, Scotlyn, my darling, there's no need to be rude. I want our union to be a happy one. That's why you're here, so we can clear the air, set some ground rules for our relationship," he waved his hand, "start fresh. After all, we're going to be together for many, *many* years, and I want them to be enjoyable for both of us."

Standing, Basil snapped his fingers and pointed at her. Scottie watched in amazement as the biggest cat she'd ever seen, with shoulders almost as wide as Marrok's and a big bald head that reminded her of Mr. Clean, jumped to attention, strode forward, sat her up, and replaced the silver on her wrists and ankles with a soft, cloth rope. Holding up her hands, the lioness raised a single eyebrow and growled, "This is your idea of civilized? Keeping me trussed up like a calf at the rodeo?"

Grinning like a villain from the comic books Piotr used to read when they were kids, Basil ran his fingers across his mustache and through his goatee before tapping his top lip and mockingly consoled, "It is for your own safety, my dear. If…"

"My own safety?" Scottie laughed sarcastically, cutting off Basil's next lie. "And how is keeping me tied up and locked away for my own safety?"

Once again snapping his fingers, this time making the tall, skinny lion with long, scraggly hair and an unkempt beard jump to attention, grab a folding chair from the corner, race back and set it down next to the cot, Basil took a seat. After making a show of unbuttoning his jacket, crossing his legs, and straightening the pleat in his pants, the wretched King nodded. "Yes, your safety." He tapped his temple then gave another single nod. "I'm a keen student of behavior and do you know what I have learned about you since entering this room?"

Scottie thought about ignoring him, or better yet, raising her feet and kicking the sorry piece of crap in the stomach, but she knew that would only end up with her back in silver and no closer to being free. Instead, she rolled her eyes and with as much disdain as possible, said, "Enlighten me."

A flicker, just a tiny spark of anger, flashed in the soulless depths of Basil's black eyes a split second before he schooled his features, forced his thin, bloodless lips into a grimace parading as a smile, and proceeded to speak to her as if she was a child.

"Your actions, dear Scotlyn, tell me that if I were to let you sit there without the ropes, you would run. My men would then be forced to chase you and in their zeal to please me by bringing you back, I fear you might be injured."

Biting the insides of her cheeks to keep from bursting out laughing, the Princess looked at the motley crew Basil called 'his men', imagining the torture she had planned for each man as punishment for his part in her abduction. She had no doubt of her ability to make them cry like babies and beg for her to stop.

Looking back at Basil, Scottie raised her bound hands and motioned with the index finger of her left hand, waiting as the bastard leaned forward. As soon as he was close enough to hear her whisper, the lioness winked, "You really should be worrying about your own ass." She chuckled. "Cause if I don't get you, Marrok sure as hell will. You can bet your furry hide, he's coming for you. I'd stake my life on it."

She could scent the fear her threat had raised in Basil, even as he tried to act coy. Leaning back, he picked a bit of imaginary lint from his trousers and chuckled. "Oh, but we will be long gone from here by the time your *wolf*," he spat the word like it tasted bad, "even thinks of waking up. My friend, Virgil," he pointed to the third idiot in his band of merry men, a short, heavyset lion with eyes as round as saucers and a nervous habit of sliding his eyes from side-to-side, "added something special to the ketamine."

Suddenly nervous, Scottie worked hard to mask her fear as she watched Basil stand, fix the collar of his jacket, and step towards her. Chills ran down her spine as he ran the backs of his fingers against her cheek and shook his head. "Poor Marrok got a little case of the Wolf's Bane flu. I hear it really is a bitch." With her chin between his thumb and forefinger, Basil forced Scottie's head back as far as it would go then leaned down until their noses almost touched and tauntingly whispered, "Your big, bad Alpha is down for the count. He won't be able to save himself, let alone you, my sweet."

Snatching his fingers from her face, the bastard took a step back, looking way more satisfied than Scottie could allow. Rage replaced terror as she jumped to her feet, teetering to maintain her balance, and ground out through gritted teeth, "I cannot wait to watch Marrok tear you limb from limb." She hopped closer. "I am going to mount your head over my mantel and make your pelt into a rug." Throwing back her head, the lioness cackled like a loon, then dropping her chin, narrowed her gaze and added with a snort, "And I'm gonna let Old Man Ferguson's pigs have the rest of you." She took another hop forward. "Because pig slop is all you're good for, Basil Reville, King of the Losers."

From one heartbeat to the next, Scottie went from precariously standing before Basil to flying through the air and landing ass over tits in the middle of the cot she'd just vacated. His roar shook the frosted windows of her prison as he flung the metal chair against the wall and bellowed, "Get the hell out," to her kidnappers. Scottie refused to cover her face or even flinch as a ceramic lamp with no shade, a small wooden table, metal step

ladder, and another folding chair were also thrown about the

room, leaving the lioness sitting among the falling debris. Gone

was Basil's perfectly constructed façade, replaced with the

lunatic Scottie knew him to be. Spittle ran down his chin and he

continued to rant.

"I will drink that wolf's blood!" he spat, grabbing the leg

of the table, still connected to the top and beating it against the

floor, punctuating every word, as he railed, "Ground..." *crash!*

His..." *smash!* "Bones..." *bang!* "To..." *crunch!* "Dust."

Bracing herself, Scottie let out the breath she'd been

holding when the last piece of wood flew from Basil's hand,

sailed over her head and splinters rained down like pieces of hail

from an angry sky. Unfortunately, she'd breathed too soon.

From one second to the next, Basil flew at her in a blind

rage. She watched his hands change to the huge paws of his beast.

Saw the points of his outstretched claws searching for her tender skin. Felt the breeze from the first swipe as he grabbed for her arm.

Rolling to her back, Scottie kicked out with her still bound feet, grazing his chest and momentarily throwing Basil off balance. Scrambling off the cot, the lioness fell onto the painted concrete floor with a painful thud before trying to get under the frame for cover.

Claws dug into the muscle of her calves. Red hot pain tore through her legs as she was yanked from under the cot, flipped over onto her back, and lifted into the air by the neck. Swinging like a ragdoll as Basil shook her until her teeth rattled in her head, Scottie's nails tore at the fur covering his paw. Gasping for air, black spots clouded her vision and tears rolled down her face as the King's grip grew tighter.

In the elliptical pupils of his lion's eyes, Scottie could see the depths of his madness as he pulled her face to his and growled through gritted teeth, "If I can't have you, then no one shall have you."

Marrok

Tightening his grip, Basil ground his lips to hers and shoved his dry, rough tongue into her mouth. Summoning the last vestiges of her strength as she drew a fleeting breath, Scottie bit down on the old bastard's tongue, smiling as he flung her limp body against the stone wall with an agonizing roar.

"That'll teach you to fuck with me," was the Princess' last thought as she succumbed to the darkness.

Chapter Seven

"**M**arrok!"

The voice sounded so far away…like a dream…but still insistent and incredibly irritating.

"Dammit, Marrok! Wake the hell up!" Louder, more demanding…closer this time, the voice bellowed.

"Finn?" the Alpha croaked, his throat dry as the Sahara and his mouth feeling like it was full of cotton.

"Yes, it's Finn. Now, get your mangy ass up off the asphalt, lunkhead, before I'm forced to dump this bucket of water over your head."

Opening one eye, Marrok warned, "One drop of that hits me and see what happens." The words had barely left his mouth when pain, like a knife splitting him open from stem to stern, tore through his body, his brain threatened to burst from his skull, and his eyes felt like ice picks were being shoved into them.

Rolling to his side and drawing up his knees in a fetal position, the Alpha clamped his lips tight, holding back the howl of unparalleled torture now tearing through his skull like a bowling ball racing down the lane. Over and over the waves of sheer agony battered his mind and body.

"Marrok! Marrok! What the fuck?" Finn bellowed.

"What's wrong, Marr?" Thane's hands touched the Alpha's shoulder, causing new shards of pain to slice through his body. The Beta with the tremendous healing powers meant well, but whatever was trying to eat its way out of Marrok's body was too strong for the young wolf.

Rolling away from his Packmates, blood pooled in his palms where the claws of his beast had broken through the ends of his fingers and ripped his skin. He felt fur growing down his back as the howl he'd been holding back burst from his lips.

His wolf pushed through the pain, forced himself to the forefront and with a tsunami of metaphysical power and intense magic stronger than anything the Alpha had ever felt, threw Marrok into a mind-numbing, spine-chilling shift. Panting, trying to pull life-affirming air into the lungs of his wolf, the Alpha opened his eyes, adjusted his perspective, and looked at his three Betas, looking on in awe.

"What the hell is that?" Errol gawked.

Moving forward with his hand held out palm-side down and his head bowed, Finn quietly replied, "This is our Alpha's Warrior form?"

"The hell you say?" Thane marveled. "Warrior doesn't do that massive wolf justice."

Still using the immense magic of his wolf to push what he'd now identified as Wolf's Bane from his body, Marrok listened as Finn explained. "Yeah, you got that right. It's one of the many things that an Alpha like him can do that we cannot. In times when either man or wolf or both are in mortal danger, their mate is being threatened, or the Pack needs defending, a True Alpha, one such as ours, can call forth this form to protect what is his."

Inching forward, Errol dropped to his knees and let his chin drop to his chest. "May I approach, Alpha?"

Yipping his approval as the last of the Wolf's Bane left his body, Marrok stood tall as the young Tracker got back to his feet and slowly moved forward. Circling the Alpha, Errol remarked, "My grandfather used to tell me stories about the special powers of a True Alpha, but I never imagined anything like this." He snickered. "I actually thought the old guy was kinda nuts."

Stepping back, he looked the giant auburn wolf in the eye and continued, "Marrok, man, you are freakin' huge. I mean, b-i-g." He spread his arms out as wide as they would go and chuckled as he swatted Thane on the shoulder with the back of his outstretched hand. "Look at that. His back is at least five feet high and his head six. He's damn near as big as a War Wolf as he is as a man."

"It's not his size that freaks me out," Thane shook his head. "It's his magic." His blue eyes grew bigger as he continued in a reverent tone, "Can't you feel it? It's like he's channeling the Goddess, the Earth…everything, *all magic*. The power is intoxicating."

"Well, while that's impressive and all, I'm still freaked out over those claws that look like talons and his extra-long canines and this is about the fiftieth time I've seen our Alpha in his 'roided-out' form." Finn was smiling but his tone was anything but jovial.

Moving out of the glare from the overhead light, sure the human patrons visiting the nearby bars would freak out seeing a wolf the size of a full-grown grizzly parading through town, the Alpha turned towards his Betas as the Hunger reared its ugly head. Need, like fire, filled his veins. Visions of Scotlyn filled his mind. His claws lengthened and his paws curled, mimicking the actions of his human hands as if they were stroking her long red curls.

Nearly dropping to the ground as memories of Scotlyn's abduction flashed into his mind, Marrok howled long and loud. His Betas, unable to resist the call of their Alpha to protect one of their own, answered his call, filling the night sky. Calling to his mate telepathically, he tried to make contact, but his call reverberated back to him as if hitting a brick wall.

The bastard is blocking our bond. If he's harmed a hair on her head, I will tear him into so many pieces, they'll be too small to burn on a funeral pyre.

Galloping past as his friends shifted to wolves, Marrok heard the distant echo of the rest of his Pack. Telepathically reassuring those he'd sworn to lead and shelter, the Alpha charged towards the one person he knew had the answers he needed.

Thundering footsteps followed closely behind as Finn's chuckle sounded in Marrok's mind, *"I'm guessing we're off to save the Princess?"*

"I would say this sounds like a Disney movie but they seriously give us wolves a bad name," Errol barked with laughter.

"Shut up, Err," Thane sighed then to Marrok, *"Do we know where she is?"*

"No, but I have a good idea who does," he growled in response, using more of his considerable power to cross the wetlands as quickly as he possibly could.

The Gaelach Lán wolves knew the swamps like the pads of their paws. A trip that would've taken nearly thirty minutes by truck, was over and done in less than ten.

Weaving past the guards like they were standing still, the wolves jumped onto the wraparound porch as one. Marrok burst through the front door, threw his head back, and scented the air before ordering, *"Down the hall. Follow me,"* before taking off to the right.

Throwing his body against the enormous oak doors, the Alpha snarled as the wood cracked and splinters flew into the air as the doors flew open. Loud screams accompanied a mighty roar as Marrok, followed by his Betas, dashed into the room, changing from wolves to men as they ran.

Stopping in front of the Lion King, the Alpha grabbed Cleander by the collar of his freshly pressed dress shirt and through gritted teeth, commanded, "Tell me where she is and we'll go in peace. Lie to me and I'll gut you where you stand."

Growls, intense and threatening, filled the room. The noxious scent of aggression and male ego burned his nose. The male lions of Pride Cattanach were closing in. Invading their home was one thing, but threatening their King was a whole new can of worms, one Marrok would never have opened had there been any other way, had the Hunger not been driving his every action…had he not been able to feel the real and present danger to his mate's life. Only his claws pushing against the tender skin over their King's jugular kept the Betas and guards at bay. One wrong move and he and his wolves would have to fight their way out of some odds that were seriously stacked against them.

Glaring at Cleander, Marrok tightened his grip ever so slightly and snarled, "Talk, King. She's your daughter and he's your rival. I know you know where she is. Don't make me do something we'll both regret to find her." He moved closer, letting his wolf show in his eyes, "Just know this," he ground out. "I will move Heaven and Hell to find her and mow down anyone who gets in my way."

A single nod from the mountain lion King had Marrok jerking his hand away and Cleander clearing his throat. Maintaining his composure, the King slowly shook his head in the direction of his second-in-command, Dilan, who looked like he wanted to rip out Marrok's spine and tie the Alpha up with it, before beginning to speak. "I see what my men have told me is true. Scotlyn has been taken. You are her true mate." The King straightened his collar and took a large gulp of whiskey before continuing, "And from the look of it, in the throes of the Hunger."

Advancing on Cleander but instead running smack into Finn's outstretched hand, Marrok roared, "Where. Is. Scotlyn?"

Closing ranks around their King, it was obvious the Betas of Pride Cattanach were just about fed up with the Alpha's show of force in their territory. Marrok looked into the eyes of some of his oldest friends. He'd known Dilan since they'd both been knee high to a grasshopper. Together with Finn, they'd caused real trouble back in the day. Piotr, the best tracker that wasn't a wolf, the Alpha had ever seen. He'd helped find Olivia the first time she ran off and hid because Marrok had pissed her off in one way or another.

Taking a deep breath, the Alpha took a step back and in the calmest voice he could muster but still growling, he asked, "Where has Basil taken her?" He blew out a quick breath. "Just tell me and I'll bring her back." He paused and then added, "Or die trying."

Turning to his men, Cleander nodded, "Everyone out but Dilan and Piotr."

A dull roar rose from the seven other lions in the room, especially the twins and their cousins, whom Marrok knew were good friends of Scotlyn's from the memories she'd shared with him. Stepping forward, Josiah, the oldest of the twins, bowed his head and asked, "Respectfully, King, my brother, Hamm and I would like to stay. We can help find Scotti...I mean, Scotlyn."

"I have no doubt of your abilities but with Dilan and Piotr about to leave the Pride, I'll need you three here to help keep the peace until my daughter is returned."

Marrok looked on, trying to hold back his roars of impatience. He applauded the King's diplomacy in a difficult situation but truly didn't give a shit. Marrrok needed to find Scotlyn. Needed her by his side. Needed to know she was safe.

Needed her more than he needed air. She was his heart and soul…his whole world, and if he didn't have her back in his arms soon, there was no telling who he'd tear apart.

Waiting until the others had gone and what was left of the door was propped up against the frame, Cleander finally pulled out a large map of the southern half of Florida. Pointing to a large parcel of farmland close to the west coast, about thirty miles from where Marrok was standing at that very moment, the King said, "This is the old Reville homestead. No one's lived there since the Elder Reville died." Anger flashed in his eyes and his voice grew gruff. "Basil had to have a new, fancy house more near the water, and my Pride's holdings." Taking a deep breath, he finished, "That's where he'll be."

Not waiting a second longer, Marrok spun on his heels and called over his shoulder, "Then that's where I'm going." Picking up the pace and calling forth the magic to transform, he added, "Let's go get us a snake in lion's fur."

Chapter Eight

"**W**hat is this, same song, second verse?" Scottie grumbled as she

 woke tied to yet another bed. The only difference was this time it felt like she was swallowing nails and the skin on her throat was on fire. Other than that, it pretty much felt like she was stuck

in a bad remake of Groundhog's Day.

Turning her head from side-to-side, the lioness took in the old fashioned flowery wallpaper, antique furniture, and stale scent of Jungle Gardenia perfume and knew immediately she was at the old Reville homestead. Not that she'd visited them much, only when forced or bribed, because Basil had been a creepy little so-and-so even at a younger age, still way older than Scottie but younger. However, she did remember his mother fondly. Beatrice Reville was a true southern lady who could trace her ancestors back to the first lion shifters who ever set paw in the Sunshine State.

One of three sisters, and the only one to marry, Miss Bea as she liked to be called, had married the Elder Reville, combining their two Prides and taking her rightful place in feline royalty. She always seemed happy and the Elder Reville doted on her like she was the sun and he was happy to live in her orbit. Then tragedy struck. A group of rogue cats hit the plantation, took out everyone in their path, and left Miss Bea to die alone, on the floor of her Florida room in a pool of her own blood.

The Elder Reville, his Beta, Basil, and most of their males returned home to find the massacre. After Miss Bea's memorial service, the Elder Reville locked himself away for nearly a year. Thankfully, his Beta was good at his position, kept the Pride running, and spent a lot of time getting Basil ready to take over. Until that time, the bastard only ranked a five out of ten on the creep-o-meter…unfortunately, things changed and not for the better.

Basil's father emerged from his self-imposed exile a cruel, bitter man. Losing the love of his life had left him cold and uncaring for anyone and anything; even his son. His sole purpose became catching the rogues who had taken his sweet mate from his life and punishing them in every way he could.

He tasked Basil with doing the same and if the younger Reville should fail, his father's reprimand was punitive, harsh, and lasted longer with each occurrence. From the stories told by the men who sought refuge within Pride Cattanach, it all came to a head when the Elder Reville attempted to string Basil up to a post and whip him with a cat-of-nine-tails. Scottie didn't know many details and didn't care, all she was sure of was that the Reville's were bad news from the ground up and she wanted no part of them. The slimy bastard may have had a fucked-up childhood, but that did not give him the right to treat her like chattel.

Lifting her hand, Scottie found restraints, not unlike those she'd seen in hospitals. It appeared the same were around her ankles, along with a three-inch wide belt across her stomach.

"Note to self, Basil is also a freak," the lioness half-laughed, half-snorted to herself. "I do *not* want to know why the sick bastard has restraints of any kind, much less in the bedroom."

Blowing the bangs out of her eyes, Scottie stared at the ceiling as she took a deep breath, counted to five, and then slowly let it out. The same nasty magic that had been in the first little concrete room was also contaminating the air in Miss Bea's bedroom, but this time, with a larger space to fill, it wasn't as strong and was dissipating by the moment.

Calling to her lioness, Scottie smiled as warm fur rubbed the underside of her skin, pushing through and covering her extremities like a thin blanket of down. Stretching her fingers, she allowed the razor-sharp claws of the beast with whom she shared her soul to replace her normally short, manicured nails.

Bending her hand at the wrist, the Princess had just begun to cut through the tough leather and thick lamb's wool of the restraints when the door to her prison flew open and in walked the lion she'd dubbed 'Mr. Clean' carrying a tray of food. Pulling back her fur and claws, Scottie smiled sweetly and mockingly cooed, "For me?"

The words had only just left her mouth when in paraded the two she'd seen earlier plus four more males and two females. "Well, hot damn, it's a party," she whooped, looking each lion in the eye, promising retribution for their part in her imprisonment.

Grunting something unintelligible, Mr. Clean slammed the tray down on the table under the window, did an about-face, and stalked towards her. Throwing off the sheet that had been covering her, he leaned down until the tips of their noses almost touched and grumbled, "Don't try anything stupid. The boss says we can take extreme measures," he grinned evilly. "Just no marks on your pretty little face." He stood up and grabbed her wrist and began unbuckling the restraint. "So, whatcha say? Wanna go a few rounds, Princess?" The last word was accompanied with enough animosity to choke a horse.

"Me against seven of you?" She scoffed. "I hardly think that's a fair fight."

Chuckling as he slapped a silver cuff on the wrist he'd just released, Mr. Clean pooh-poohed, complete with a fake pout, "Oh no, poor little Princess afraid?"

Pausing until he looked up at her, Scottie raised her head from the pillow and sneered, "I meant…" She winked. "Not fair for y'all."

Using the knuckles on the back of her hand that Mr. Clean so readily held in the air, Scottie punctuated her retort with a quick punch to his nose. She heard the crack of his bones a split second before blood spurted from his face like a fountain. Howling with pain, Mr. Clean dropped her hand and spun around in circles while the rest of his crew closed in around where the Princess lay laughing out loud.

Grabbing the sheet Mr. Clean had thrown at the end of the bed, the female mountain lion with short platinum curls and deep violet eyes scowled in Scottie's direction as she grabbed the bald idiot by the arm, forced him into the chair by the table, and began applying pressure to his broken nose. The second female, a lioness Scottie'd had the distinct displeasure of dealing with before, Mona, moved to the other side of the bed and began undoing the restraint on that wrist.

"Don't do anything stupid, Scotlyn, you'll only make matters worse…but then that's your m.o. isn't it?"

Shaking her head, Scottie rolled her eyes as she sighed. "Ya' know, if I recall correctly, it was you and your group of mean girls who made things worse. Didn't your momma tell you that drinking with coyotes always leads to trouble?" She feigned shock, complete with wide eyes and a gasp, then added mock pity. "Oh, I'm so sorry, I forgot, you and your momma don't get along, do ya'?"

Rage burned like red hot coals in Mona's deep blue eyes as she growled, "Leave my mother out of this."

Grinning like the Cheshire cat from Alice in Wonderland, Scottie snickered, "Did I hit a nerve?"

Before the Princess could blink, Mona slapped her across the face and had her hand raised to do it again. Thankfully, her efforts were thwarted when a tall, lanky lion with shaggy, dirty blonde hair sped across the room and grabbed the angry lioness by the wrist. "Not in the face, Mona," he warned in a low, threatening tone. "Get back over there. Let me do this. Basil's gonna be waitin' and I'm not gonna get another ass chewin' for your fuck-up."

Ignoring the sting on her cheek, Scottie laughed, "Yeah, Mona. Go on, now, run along. We all know you screw up damn near everything you touch." She blew a kiss. "I'll tell your momma you said hi."

Scottie knew she was being a bitch and egging the female on, talking about her mother. It was well known throughout Pride Cattanach that Mona's mother, Felicia, had begged Cleander to exile her daughter instead of putting her to death for the part she played in her father's death. They never proved she actually pushed him off that cliff, but there was concrete evidence that Mona had been the one to lure him up to the Pointe where he was ambushed by a Band of Coyotes.

The ones responsible for Mannick's death had been beheaded, but after almost three days of deliberating with his Betas, Cleander granted Felicia's wish and Mona was sent away with the edict never to return or face a death sentence. It was no surprise to Scottie that the bitch had taken up with Basil. She'd even hoped he'd mate Mona and leave her alone, but some wishes just never come true.

The scraggily lion made quick work of Scottie's restraints and clamped cotton-lined cuffs on her wrists, throwing the one Mr. Clean had put on her wrist earlier to the side. He then put matching shackles connected by a chain on her ankles before pulling her off the bed and forcing her to stand at his side.

"Stand right there, Princess," he grumbled. "We'll be heading down in just a minute."

"But, don't I get to eat?"

Just gotta poke the lion... I swear it's a character flaw, but, damn it's fun...

"Hell no!" Came Mr. Clean's muddled reply from the other side of the room.

Looking to the side, Scottie saw the female taking care of him had gotten the bleeding stopped by stuffing pieces of ripped sheet up his nose. The Princess wanted to burst out laughing but the mangy lion's grip on her arm tightened to the point of pain when he saw her smirk as Mr. Clean continued griping, "I hope you starve." Then he stood and gave her a jagged grimace around his swollen nose and split lip. "Or Basil beats the shit out of you during the Mating Ceremony."

Hiding her shock behind another sarcastic comment, Scottie snorted, "Not likely. I hear he hasn't got the right stuff." She lifted her pinky finger, wiggled it up and down, and shrugged.

The fingers around her arm grew ever tighter. She could feel the bruises rising under her skin. Her lioness issued a threatening growl, pushing against the confines of Scottie's mind, spoiling for a fight.

The asshole shoved her forward. The whole room erupted in laughter as Scottie fell onto her knees, the rough edges of the tile cutting into her palms. The female who'd patched up Mr. Clean pulled the Princess to her feet and glared at the others.

"Basil also said no blood." She stepped up to the scraggily lion, "So, I guess you'll be paying for your fuck-up."

The male closed the scant distance between them with a menacing growl. "Fuck off, Amanda," he spat, shoving past her and storming out of the room.

"Grab her other arm." Amanda nodded to a young male who looked scared out of his wits.

Hesitantly moving forward, the young male's whiskey-colored eyes flashed to Scottie's. She could see the fear in his eyes and scent his regret at being a part of what was happening to her. Smiling sincerely at him as he gently placed his hand around her upper arm, the Princess gave a tiny nod to let the Cub know she appreciated the difficulty of his situation.

I hope he gets out of this shit alive…

As for the rest of them, she hoped they died slow, painful, horrible deaths and she prayed she was there to see the light fade from their eyes. Keeping in step with Amanda and the young male, Scottie tried to remember the layout of the house as just the three of them, along with Shaggy, as she'd started thinking of the long-haired lion, who was bringing up the rear, took a right after exiting Miss Bea's room.

"Be sure to keep a close eye on her," Mona scoffed. "I wouldn't wanna have to chase her down." Scottie could not wait to slap the snarkiness out of that murderous bitch, but first, the Princess had to escape.

Winding through the upper floor of the huge plantation home, she remembered a back staircase that divided into two about halfway down. One side went into the kitchen, the other led to a huge pantry with an exit to the outside. Shuffling along like a prisoner on death row, the Princess smiled to herself as they stopped at the top of the stairs. Her smile only widened when the young male knelt down and removed the shackles from her ankles.

Standing, he started down the stairs as Amanda snapped and pointed, "Now, you, Princess," before taking her place behind, with Shaggy still playing caboose.

Taking a deep breath, Scottie slowly let it out, counting down from three in her mind. No sooner had she thought of the number one then she stepped onto the landing where the stairway split. Taking full advantage of the narrow nineteenth-century stairway, Scotty pushed the young male forward, spinning on her toes and flattening her back against the wall as he tumbled down the stairs.

Ducking just as Amanda reached for her, the Princess swung her arms against the female's legs, giving them a little extra push as Amanda flew forward to be sure she didn't get up. Throwing herself onto her back, Scottie grunted as the steps dug into her spine. Kicking out with her feet, she caught Shaggy in the side as he lunged for her then watched as he fell forward, hitting his head on the solid mahogany banister and sliding down the stairs to join his cohorts in a pile of unconscious lions.

Jumping to her feet, Scottie raced down the stairs, over her inept captors, and into the pantry. Slamming the large wooden door shut, she pushed the old brass hook lock into the catch before twirling around and running for the outside door. Fumbling with the updated bolt lock, she cursed the cuffs those bastards had put on her as it finally clicked open. Turning the nob, she smiled as she felt the cool evening air and the last rays of the setting sun hit her face.

Stepping out onto the wooden steps, she pulled the door shut, turned, and ran headlong into Basil. Looking up into the black, soulless eyes of the last person on earth she wanted to see, dread filled her soul as the stupid son of a bitch, tsked, "Now, now, now, my dear. You shouldn't be running about so close to dark." He pulled her tight to his chest, tightening his arms around her to the point of pain and making it hard for her to breathe while trapping her arms.

Struggling for air, Scottie knew she was going to pass out, actually prayed for it as Basil droned on and on. Then just as she became lightheaded, the Princess heard the most glorious sound, Marrok's voice, loud and clear in her mind.

"Hang on, mo kitten milis. I'm coming for ya' and Goddess help the fucking bastard who took you."

Chapter Nine

Reaching the outskirts of the old Reville homestead, Marrok stopped just long enough to open his wolf senses, count twenty lions guarding the perimeter of the fifty-acre plantation, and find a dead spot on the banks of a lake at the back of the property.

That's where he's taking her…

The words were still crossing his mind when Marrok took off running across the backside of the estate. Normally cool and calm, a master tactician, the Alpha was losing all control. The Hunger was driving him to be reckless. His fiery need for Scotlyn was burning a hole through his soul. The long sharp claws of this Ancient Curse were ripping him to shreds from the inside-out. The few words he'd gotten to speak to her before she'd lost consciousness had only fed the Hunger, pushed Marrok farther from sanity.

I will gut that stupid son of a bitch...

Trying to focus, the sounds of wolf and lion paws on his heels pushed the Alpha to nearly double his speed. Rationally, he knew it was only his Betas along with Cattanach's, but his wolf, the one obviously running the show, would not...*could not* let anyone get to his mate before he did. Scotlyn needed him. The Goddess only knew what Reville had planned. He was old and devious and more than anything else, truly evil.

"Marrok, you gotta stop and think. You can't go in there half-cocked. That won't do Scottie any good," Finn's voice sounded in the Alpha's mind.

"Have. To. Save. Her."

"I know and we will, but please let us help you."

Ignoring his Beta's pleas, as well as the others' concerns he could feel bombarding his raw senses, Marrok pushed on. Coming to a screeching halt on the far side of the boathouse when he could finally scent Scotlyn, the Alpha counted eight lions, including Basil, standing around his mate. Diving into the tall sawgrass and cattails on the banks of the lake, he crawled on his belly, making his way closer still.

Finally, close enough to get a good look at Scotlyn, it took all the control he had left plus the power he felt his Betas pouring into him to stay. Not only was she unconscious and chained to a large flat stone in the center of a Sacred Circle, but his lioness was also completely naked. The claws of his warrior form lengthened, digging into the soft sandy soil. He wore a snarl, his long canines ready to tear the flesh from Basil.

Finn, Thane, and Errol arrived behind him. The strength they shared with him continued as his Beta explained, *"The lions have gone around to strike from the other side. We're all just waiting on you to give the order."*

Long seconds ticked by while Marrok tried to think through the raw power of the Hunger long enough to come up with some semblance of a plan that wouldn't end up with any of his people or Cattanach's getting hurt. It was no use. The longer

Scotlyn lay there silent, still…naked, the harder it was for him to think of anything but getting her out of harm's way and ridding the world of the blight known as Basil Reville.

Preparing to pounce, Marrok's heart beat double time as the soft sound of Scotlyn's sleepy mumble reached his ears. He wanted to howl his thanks to the Goddess when she turned her head and looked right at him, a small smile curving her beautiful lips.

Lowering his snout, the Alpha whispered, *"I'm here, mo kitten."*

"Never had a doubt, mo alfa." The soft murmur of his lioness' soft voice pushed back a bit of the madness, giving Marrok enough of his sanity to see a plan and relay it to the others.

Waiting until everyone was in place, Marrok changed from wolf to man and with the grandeur that only a true Alpha can provide, rose out of the tall grass at the edge of the water and bellowed, "Release Scotlyn and all will be forgiven, Reville."

Spinning around like he was riding a merry-go-round, Basil hid the fear Marrok saw shining in his eyes with an incredible show of bravado clearly meant to inspire the members of his Pride. "Well, lookie what we have here. Is that a wolf on Pride lands?" The bastard stepped closer to Scotlyn. "Remind me, Marrok," he drew out the Alpha's name sarcastically, "what is the penalty for trespassing?"

Stepping forward, Marrok stopped just outside the circle of small rocks, slid his feet shoulder width apart, and crossed his arms over his bare chest. Shaking his head, the Alpha shrugged. "I have no clue what your penalty is, nor do I care." He looked at each lion who had stepped up to the circle then nodded, "But I know that the penalty for kidnapping and torture is death." He gave a single chuckle. "And since it's *my mate*," he stared at Basil as he emphasized the words one more time, "*my woman*, I promise it will be slow and painful."

127

The acrid scent of fear filled the air, so strong and pungent that it overpowered the pleasant aroma of burning cedar. Confidence was waning in Basil's ranks. One more push and Marrok had no doubt most of them would abandon the fight in order to save their own hides.

"Your woman?" Basil taunted as he ran the tips of his fingers over Scotlyn's bare torso. "It looks like she's with me."

The Alpha's feet moved forward of their own volition. Finn and Dilan's screams simultaneously burst through his mind.

"Stop! Marrok! Wait!"

Using every ounce of strength he had, the Alpha stood perfectly still, barely breathing, and held back the raging warrior wolf within him before asking, "Why don't we ask her? Let Scotlyn make her own decision."

Sneering at Marrok's suggestion, Basil clamped down on Scotlyn's breast, squeezing until his hand shook from the exertion. The Alpha's eyes darted to his mate's. Tears ran down her cheek as she bit her lip to keep from crying out.

Rage tore through Marrok like a runaway train. His hard-fought control torn to shreds as he roared, "You. Will. Die."

Chaos erupted. Their plan was shot to hell. Half the lions of Pride Reville were shifting to fight, the rest were scattering like rats from a sinking ship. Flying at Basil, Marrok changed from man to wolf in the blink of an eye. His front paws crashed into Basil's chest as the bastard was mid-transformation.

Landing on all fours, Marrok spun around just as Basil, in lion form, lunged towards him. Knocking him away, the Alpha focused on Scotlyn's screams, knew she was struggling to free herself, and quickly reassured, *"I'm coming as soon as I send this bastard to Hell."*

"That stupid piece of shit is mine. You can knock him down but I get to send him to Hell," she demanded.

"As you wish, mo bhanríon."

The two mighty beasts squared off. Circling to the right, sure to maintain eye contact with his mortal enemy, Marrok tried to close the distance between he and the coward who dared to touch his Scotlyn.

Listening to the snarling behind him, the Alpha kept his mind wide open to not only his mate, but also his compatriots. Any other time he would've laughed at the comments flying back and forth between his Betas and Dilan as they toyed with Reville's poorly trained and lazy lions.

Knowing his friends had the rest of the battle well in hand, Marrok returned all of his focus to Basil. Fear and rage shined brightly in the dark eyes of the large mountain lion. The Alpha lunged forward with a loud snarl and show of teeth. The lion scooted to the side, stepping back…trying to escape.

"Get behind Basil, Finn," Marrok ordered, sure the others could handle the remaining mountain lion who, from the sound of things, was trying to run away.

Marrok

"Sure thing, Boss."

Lunging again as his Beta got into position, the Alpha wanted to laugh out loud as Basil roared and made a show out of standing on his hind legs while swatting at Marrok's face with his razor-sharp claws. Ignoring the pain of Basil's strikes, the Alpha leapt forward, biting into the huge mountain lion's soft underbelly, ripping out a large chunk of flesh with a loud snarl.

Roaring in pain, Basil fell forward, barely landing on all fours. Quickly regaining his footing, the lion King dove forward, a snarling mass of fangs and claws aiming for Marrok's neck. Stepping to the side, the Alpha ran headlong into the lion's flank, throwing him into Finn, who shoved his front paws into Basil's opposite side and catapulted the mountain lion into the side of the large flat stone where Scotlyn continued to struggle with her chains.

Leaping into the air, Marrok landed upon Basil, his massive front paws on the mountain lion's chest forced the King onto his back as the Alpha's mouth closed over his enemy's neck.

The King struggled with the last of his waning strength, slashing his claws in rapid succession down both sides of Marrok's soft underbelly. The lion King froze as the Alpha pushed the tips of his large canines into the soft tissue of Basil's throat.

"Free Scotlyn," Marrok commanded.

Finn leapt onto the rock, changing back to his human form in midair, and quickly released Scotlyn. Marrok watched as from one second to the next his gorgeous mate became the beautiful lioness who had first called to him and his wolf. Leaping from her perch, the Princess growled, *"Let me at him, Marrok. I need to finish this."*

"He's all yours," the Alpha quickly answered, slowly loosening the hold he had on the lion's neck.

In one last show of force, Basil tried to jump to his feet as Marrok raised his snout, but Scotlyn was too quick. Bounding forward, she pounced on the King, dug her claws into his chest, and roared in his face.

"Lay down and die, you sorry son of a bitch." The power and magic in her words so powerful that not only did it ring through Marrok's mind, but he also saw the recognition in Dilan's lion's and in those of his Betas'.

"Mercy. Please show mercy on me, Scotlyn." Marrok listened to the King beg through his mental connection to Scotlyn.

"Mercy?" She slashed her nails across the hole Marrok had left in the lion's stomach, chuckling in her own mind as Basil whimpered in pain. *"I owe you nothing."* She dug her nails into his wound and snarled, *"I am glad you're going to Hell, because I would hate for your mother to see how you turned out."*

The claws of her right paw dug deeper as blood wet not only Basil's fur but also the ground. Marrok watched as the talons on Scotlyn's left paw grew longer, sliding between the King's ribs, driving towards his lung. The Alpha knew the moment she'd hit pay dirt when Basil's whimpers turned to tortured yowls and the sound of air escaping the lion's chest like helium from the hole in a balloon filled the night sky.

Marrok watched as Scotlyn sat muzzle to muzzle, looking into the eyes of the man who'd kidnapped and tortured her then tied her to a rock. He stared as his mate dug deeper still into her enemy's chest and gullet from both sides, unable to look away as her paws and forearms disappeared inside Basil's body cavity. The Alpha literally held his breath when Scotlyn growled, *"Now, bastard, die...die and go to Hell,"* at the precise moment she heaved not only her paws, but also Basil's heart, lungs, and a few ribs from his body with a mighty roar.

Throwing the mass of bone, flesh, and blood to the sky, Scotlyn threw back her beautiful head and roared again, this time louder and with infinitely more feeling. Dilan joined in the revelry as the wolves howled their congratulations at a hard-fought victory.

Stalking over to his mate, Marrok rubbed his snout along her muzzle, licking the blood of their enemy from her face.

Marrok

Scotlyn purred low in her throat, scenting the massive warrior wolf with the side of her muzzle. Running his muzzle the length of her body on both sides as his Princess did the same, Marrok murmured, *"You were amazing, mo kitten milis, simply amazing."*

"You're not so bad yourself. I'm liking the big, bad wolf suit. I'd like to see a lot more of him," she chuckled. *"Hell, I wanna see all of you, any way I can get you, every day, forever."*

"I couldn't have said it better."

Chapter Ten

It had been five days since Scottie had laid waste to the man

 hellbent on destroying her life and officially accepted Marrok's proposal, which had been a formality her father had demanded. To say life had gotten complicated was the

understatement of the century, but for the first time in her whole

life, Scottie was happy, blissfully, complete-with-goofy-grin

happy, and there was no going back.

Because she was the one to kill Basil, it was discussed

that she would be the Queen of Pride Reville, but for Scottie, that

was a no-go. She was about to become the Alpha cat to her Alpha

wolf, making every blessed thing perfect in her world, and there

was no way she was about to give that up for a bunch of mangy

cats. So, she proposed that Pride Cattanach absorb what was left

of the mountain lions formerly loyal to Basil who would pledge

their allegiance to Cleander and the rest be exiled from the state of Florida. The Pride Council had agreed and slowly, it was coming to pass.

The rest of the time she'd been explaining to her Pride that she and Marrok would be performing the Mating Ritual of his people and that at a later date, they would do the more traditional mountain lion ritual that included a ceremony and attendance by the Elders from the Pride Council. It was shocking that her father had readily agreed while her friends, specifically Dilan, Piotr, and the twins, were the most opposed.

"Are you serious, Scots? That's just wrong." Piotr shook his head, his disgust obvious by his frown. "What are you just forgetting who you are running across the swamp to play wolf in lion's fur?"

Trying not to laugh at her friend's unintended joke, Scottie closed the distance between them and stood next to Piotr, knocking her shoulder into his. "Hey, come on, do you really believe I would leave y'all? Forget who I am? Where I come from?"

"No, I guess not."

"Besides, I thought you liked Marrok. I know you've been drinking with Finn and Thane for years." She bumped his shoulder again. "So, what's really going on?"

"He thinks you're gonna forget him," Dilan teased in a sing-songy voice.

"Shut the hell up, dick," Piotr threw back. "You're just as upset as I am. You just think you have to act tough." Then he turned to Sampson and Josiah. "And what about you two? Cat got your tongue? You afraid to appear soft and caring like the big lug over there?"

"Naw, we just want Scottie to be happy." Sampson nodded as Josiah continued, "She's only across the swamp and Marrok said after their honeymoon we can come over as often as we like."

"And the women there are hot as hell," Sampson added, complete with a blush.

Throwing his hands in the air, Piotr groaned. "Whatever, it's obvious I'm beaten." He wrapped his arm around the lioness and pulled her close. "But I swear if you start howling, I'm knocking you unconscious and dragging you back to Pride lands."

"Arrooooooo…," Scottie howled as the room erupted in laughter.

Later that day, she was just putting the finishing touches on her makeup when a knock sounded at the door. Taking one final look, she turned the knob and grinned as her father nodded and smiled, "Time to go, sweetheart. You don't want to keep that big dumb wolf of yours waiting."

"Daddy," she teased, swatting Cleander's shoulder as he laughed out loud.

"You know I had to mess with you one last time before I have to call him son."

"And so, you have," Scottie snickered.

"I have to admit, and it pains me to do so, that for a wolf, your Marrok is not a half bad guy. Not a mountain lion and not who I ever thought I would want for you, but who am I to question the Goddess." He hugged her close. "Oh, and I'm kinda happy he saved your life."

Laughing out loud, the Princess kissed her father on the cheek and teased, "I'll be sure to tell him."

Walking down the stairs, she breathed in the wonderful scent of fresh forest and male wolf. Stepping down onto the tile floor, it was all she could do to not run into Marrok's arms as he stood waiting by the front door. Walking alongside her dad, Scottie stared deep into her Alpha's eyes as they shared visions of exactly what they planned to do to one another once they were alone. With her heart racing and her body already hot with desire, Scottie leaned to the side as her father kissed her on the cheek and placed her hand into Marrok's.

Marrok

"Live well, live long, and live happy, my only daughter," Cleander reiterated the traditional lion Mating Blessing as the couple turned as one and stepped out into the cool night air.

"I can't wait much longer, Scottie. I'm hanging on by a thread," Marrok's voice floated through her mind.

She could feel the Hunger riding him hard, pushing him to complete the final step of mating. Scottie tugged on his arm and when he leaned down, she kissed the tender spot behind his ear and whispered, "Then what are you waiting for."

In the blink of an eye, Marrok scooped her off the ground and took off across the swamps and marshes that separated Pride Lands from Pack Lands. Heading into the deeper part of the forest behind his home, her Alpha stopped only when they had reached the clearing he'd shown her yesterday. Unlike when she'd seen it before, the area was now completely free of leaves and branches, covered in a blanket of rose petals with the flames of candlelight dancing from their perch atop a large stone.

What had been a small ache for the better part of the last five days was now a mass of undeniable wanton desire and the need to feel Marrok moving within her, filling her as only he could. She needed to feel his lips on her skin and his teeth at her neck, needed to be in every way the Goddess intended as soon as possible.

Looking up at her wolf as his feet touched the rose petals, Scottie sighed. "Thank you so much. This is beautiful."

Scottie slid down Marrok's body as his arms slipped from under her legs. She watched with barely contained excitement as her Alpha tore the shirt from his body. The tips of the claws of her lioness pushed through her fingertips as she closed the distance between them. Running her claws down his chest, she marked her mate for all to see and spoke the Mating words that would draw them even closer together. "Let these scratches, marks of my possession of Marrok Kilbride, be the first blood I draw from him, not in anger but as a sign to the Goddess that this is the man I love and desire above all other and there shall never be another."

Her fingers fumbled with the button at his waist while he tore the clothing from her body. Finally, both naked and completely open to one another, Marrok held his hand out for her to watch as he let the claws of his wolf extend from his fingertips.

Pulling her close, he gently drew the tips of his talons from the top of her back to her bottom, leaving a fiery trail down her back and intense need filling her body. Looking deep into her eyes, he repeated the Mating words. "Let these scratches, marks of my possession and a promise to always protect Scotlyn Cattanach, be the first blood I draw from her, not in anger but as a sign to the Goddess that this is the woman I love and desire above all other and there shall never be another."

The words were still ringing in the air as Marrok lifted her into his arms and strode across the meadow to a pallet of blankets she hadn't seen until that moment. Slowly setting her onto the ground, he laid his lips to hers and in the most soul-shattering kiss, completely turned Scottie's brain to mush as he lowered them onto the pallet.

Tearing her lips from his and gasping for air, Scottie got on her knees, and after throwing her long strawberry-blonde curls over her shoulder, looked into the glowing green eyes of her Alpha and demanded, "Marrok Kilbride, take me like you own me. Love me now and please for the dear Goddess' sake, love me forever as I will love you until my dying breath and beyond. Mark me as yours, for I am all yours, heart, soul, and beast."

His deep penetrating stare as he moved behind her, his fingers kneading the cheeks of her ass, and his cock pressed against her wet, throbbing pussy was all the answer Scottie needed. Pushing back, she growled as he stopped her from forcing his erection into her needy body. Glaring at him as he ordered, "Slow down. I'm too close to losing control."

"Fuck control. I need you...just as you…" Her words were cut off as Marrok shoved three fingers deep inside her and began thrusting in and out with powerful strokes, bending the tips of his fingers, teasing the sensitive bundle of nerves at the top of her channel with every swipe.

Higher and higher her arousal grew, the proof wetting the inside of her thigh. Mindless with lust and more in love than she had ever imagined possible, Scottie rode Marrok's hand as she wanted to ride the man himself. Rocking on her knees, she met him stroke for stroke, the need to climax becoming overwhelming.

Struggling to breathe, the lioness rolled her hips at the same time her mate pushed his thumb against her throbbing clit. An orgasm of epic proportions burst from inside her. Stars filled her vision. Her own screams filled the meadow as Marrok pushed her higher and higher, only stopping his sensual assault when her head fell forward onto her hands.

Tiny shivers racked her body as her mate slowly removed his fingers and teased her opening with the tip of his cock. Once again, desire bloomed anew within her. It was as if the last few minutes had never happened. Her body longed to be one with its mate; needed to feel him filling her, loving her, making her whole as no one ever could.

Marrok's fingers bit into her waist. His breathing turned to panting as inch by inch, he worked his erection into her contracting body. Scottie's arms shook, her legs quaked, and her pussy pulled her Alpha deeper into her body until finally, she felt the tip of his cock against the mouth of her womb.

Sighing as one, the couple held still for several heartbeats, savoring their connection. Scottie had never felt so complete, so loved, so fulfilled in all her years. Her heart soared as Marrok's emotions mirrored hers and he whispered in the language of his ancestors, *"Raibh aon rud riamh álainn sin."*

Pulling back until only the head of his erection remained within her, Marrok thrust back into her over and over and over again, until only the sounds of the couple loving one another could be heard. Scottie screamed Marrok's name again and again, like a song of praise to the Goddess who had created such a perfect man for her to love.

Marrok

Leaning forward, Marrok covered her body with his while his hands cupped her swaying breasts, kneading her already hardened nipples to almost painful points as his cock drove in and out of her. Pain mixed with pleasure. Scottie was lost to all that they were together. She was complete in every way she could ever hope to be. Her claws dug into the blankets as she felt another climax roaring to its completion.

Marrok's cock buried deep inside her, his hands on her breasts and his lips at her neck sent the Princess into sensual overload. She wailed, "Now, Marrok, now! Bite me! Mark me! Make me yours!"

Meeting her Alpha thrust for thrust, Scottie screamed her orgasm to the stars above as Marrok's canines broke the tender skin at the base of her neck and he roared his release against her skin. It was nothing short of explosive and all together miraculous. The world around her went from bursts of colorful lights to total darkness that only the feel of Marrok kissing away the sting of his bite brought her back from.

Moaning at the loss as he let his still semi-erect cock slide from her body, Scottie immediately sighed as Marrok's strong arms lifted her from her knees and laid her onto her back. Finally working up the strength to open her eyes, the lioness smiled as she gazed into the eyes of her Alpha, her mate, *her forever*. The tips of her fingers traced the gentle curve of the satisfied smile that graced his kissable lips.

Her body tingled where his fingers danced across her cooling flesh as she felt the Hunger that had been pushing her mate to insanity slowly slide away. Scottie touched the mark Marrok had left on her skin. Her eyes slid shut as the scent of their love making filled her senses and her lioness purred within the confines of her mind to have been claimed by its wolf.

Only Marrok's soft masculine chuckle shook her from the euphoria. "Don't go to sleep, *mo bhanríon,* I belief you still have work to do." He tapped his neck and cleared his throat. "Notice anything missing."

Grinning like the cat that loved the wolf, Scottie pulled her big, bad Alpha's lips to hers and as she kissed him with all the love in her heart, chuckled directly into his mind, *"We have all night, my love… we have all night."*

The End (for now…)

Julia Mills

A Wolf's Hunger Series

AVAILABLE NOW!

Rafe: A K Michaels

Kade: A K Michaels

Saint: Bella Roccaforte

AX: Monica La Porta

Her Highlander's Desire: A K Michaels

Zohar: A K Michaels

COMING SOON!

Finn: Julia Mills

Holt: Desiree A. Cox

Shade: A K Michaels

Daire: Julia Mills

Brick: Elaine Barris

Tatum: S. Raven Storm

Cheveyo: Kristina Canady

Savage: Audra Hart

Roman: Desiree A. Cox

FINN: A Wolf's Hunger

Coming Soon

Life turns on a dime…

One minute up, the next down…

When there's nowhere to turn, all you can do it fight…

Finn Blakesley never wanted to lead. Coming from a family of First Betas, he was happy backing up his best friend and Alpha, Marrok Kilbride, but just when he thought he had it all figured out, The Hunger struck and nothing else mattered.

Insatiable Appetite…

Gut-wrenching Desire…

Fire-burning Bloodlust…

And it all began with just one look from a sexy she-wolf.

More wolf than man, he's on the hunt. Becky has no idea what she's unleashed but she's about to find out. The sassy little female will be his and to hell with anyone who thinks otherwise. Rogues be damned. Let 'em come. This Beta turned Alpha knows what he wants and has no problem taking it.

This isn't about Fate or Destiny… This is A Wolf's Hunger, It Cannot Be Stopped.

Get yours on AMAZON or with Kindle Unlimited!

Marrok

HER DRAGON TO SLAY

Check Out the One that Started It All for the Dragon Guard

Dragon Guard Book #1

FREE ON ALL RETAILERS

Sassy and stubborn have gotten Kyndel through everything life had to throw at her. Will her moxie help when destiny falls at her feet?

Hundreds of years of loyalty to Dragon Guard have made Rayne a fearless leader. When the long-foretold pull of his mate rocks the Commander's world to its core, will he be able to save her from his enemies in time?

The chemistry between this strong-willed curvy girl and fierce warrior makes all the difference in the world where nothing is as it seems. The existence of an ancient race of honor-clad, tradition-bound protectors might be hard to accept, but now the dead are coming back to life and holding a knife to her neck. Can these fated mates defeat their greatest enemies and get their

Julia Mills

happily ever after?

Fate Will Not Be Denied!!

Available on AMAZON, AMAZON UK, NOOK,

iBOOKS, KOBO or any retailer worldwide.

CAUGHT: A Vampire Blood Courtesan Romance

Available Now on Amazon

She trusted him with her future. How could she have known it was her heart she had to protect...

I know stealing is wrong, but those poor, forgotten children needed my help.

I had no other choice. For a few short weeks, I made a real difference.

But my luck ran out. In the blink of an eye, I went from an angel of mercy to a mouse caught in a trap.

Now, I have a choice to make...give up everything I've ever known or trust a vampire to make it all go away.

He says he can give me back my life, my career...everything I've worked so hard to achieve.

But there's a price...

In a world where blood is a commodity and sex is the prize, this cold, aloof vampire is my only way out...or is he?

The Vampire Blood Courtesans.

It's not supposed to be about love...until it is.

Available on AMAZON or with Kindle Unlimited.

Marrok

OUT OF THE ASHES

Guardians of the Zodiac, Book #1

A Zodiac Shifters Paranormal Romance

AVAILABLE NOW

Meet the Guardian of the Zodiac and introducing the

Dragon Guard of the Sea!

Lost and thought dead, these mighty dragons arise from

the depths to not only help to save all mankind, but reunite with

others of their kind.

The mission is simple – get into the enemy camp, free the

humans, return the demons to Hell, and return home the victor.

For a Daughter of Poseidon and her constant companion, Drákon

– a centuries old water dragon, that's called a good day at work.

Everything is going as planned. Una, eldest daughter and

Guardian of Pisces, has checked one and two off her list, and is

headed to three when things get complicated. Brody Mason bows

at her feet, pledging his allegiance to not only her, but also the gods and the Light. As a show of loyalty, he promises to take her to the portal from Hell and with his own blood, help her close the door on the Underworld. This one act will rid the world of evil forever. There's only one problem…he's a Hellhound.

It doesn't matter that Drákon doesn't believe him, fearing it yet another trick of Hades to deter them from their mission, or that there's fire in his eyes and the smell of brimstone on his olive skin, she can feel the truth in his words. It also doesn't hurt that with just one glance he sets her heart ablaze and her pulse racing. Not that this is about love or lust, it is all about saving the Earth, protecting the humans, defeating her uncle's evil…or is it?

One leap of faith leads Una and Brody on a race against time and facing the fight of their lives. Hiding from Poseidon, Hades, and an army of Guardians led by her sister, Zoe, this couple may have the best intentions, but in the end, isn't that what paves the road to Hell?

Available on AMAZON, AMAZON UK, NOOK, iBOOKS and KOBO!

LOLA: A 'Not-Quite' Witchy Love Story

(Magic and Mayhem Kindle World)

Available Now

Being single in a world where everything is thorn-covered roses and bags of bloody bones sucks! Heidi's got Hunter, Bert's got Luci…hell, even Lucifer's got Trixie, and then there's me, the sexiest alter ego this side of Purgatory… stuck inside a Hellhound who's happier than a zombie at the body farm in her newly wedded bliss. Sure, Heidi and her Hunkie Hellhound hump like rabbits getting ready for Easter, but even that's gotten boring. I need to get out, see the Underworld, sow my wild oats. I mean, a girl's gotta get hers while the gettin's good, am I right?

It's taken six long months of bitchin'… I mean persuading, but Heidi's finally agreed to let me have a body of my own. So, it's back into the Lady Bug Express and off to West Virginia, but this time we're avoiding the crazy Aunties and heading straight for Asscrack. Zelda, the next Baba Yaga and

Almighty Shifter Wanker, has agreed to help. She plans to yank me outta Heidi and shove me into a fresh new body before the next full moon. Then it's bingo bango, Lola's gonna get her groove on.

It looks like I might even end up with some powers. Seems Katie, the chickie whose skin will now be mine, was a witch before she hocused when she should have pocused. I might have to sidestep her sisters and hideout from some vamps, but it'll all be worth it. Imagine the possibilities... me with magic. I'm positively giddy at the idea.

The plan is flawless. I mean, come on, what could go wrong?

Grab your copy on Amazon!

ACHILLES: Soul of Her King

Available Now

A scream in the night. A panicked call for help. There's no time to think. The rules be damned.

A fate worse than death. Buried alive...lost...alone...

A centuries old secret her only hope. May the gods be on her side.

This one's about more than brotherhood.

Save the girl...save the Kings.

Get your copy on Amazon.

About Julia

Hey Y'all! I'm Julia Mills, the New York Times and USA Today Bestselling Author of the Dragon Guard Series. I without a doubt admit to being a sarcastic, southern woman who would rather spend all day laughing than a minute crying. Living with my two most amazing daughters and a menagerie of animals keeps me busy but I love telling a good story. Now, that I've decided to write the stories running through my brain, life is just a blast!

My beliefs are simple. A good book along with shoes, makeup, and purses will never let a girl down and no hero ever written will compare to my real-life hero...my dad! I'm a sucker for a happy ending and alpha men make me swoon.

I'm still working on my story but I promise it will contain as much love and laughter as I can pack into it! Now, go out there and create your own story!!! Dare to Dream! Have the Strength to Try EVERYTHING! Never Look Back!

I ABSOLUTELY adore stalkers so look me up on Facebook – Julia Mills, Author and sign up for my newsletter at JuliaMillsAuthor.com. Send me a message!

Thank you for reading my stories!!!

XOXO Julia

P.S. All my books are available on Amazon and some on other retailers, too!

Happy Reading!

Julia Mills

Printed in Poland
by Amazon Fulfillment
Poland Sp. z o.o., Wrocław